W9-BHY-418

Dear Reader,

I wrote *Want Some Get Some* during the Los Angeles riots. After the Rodney King beating, L.A. was seething. Some people took that rage to the streets. Also during this time, another famous video was circulating around. Jayne Kennedy, the Halle Berry of her day, was an actress, model, and TV personality whose image was shattered after a videotape of her was leaked—the first "sex tape" in L.A. It was a devastating fall from grace, which ruined her career.

Trudy's character was inspired by Kennedy's ordeal. I wanted to create a female character who was viciously exploited by a salacious tape. How would it make her feel? What would she do to get back at her ex Lil Steve, who sells her image?

All the characters in this story have something stripped away, which dramatically affects how they live. After the videotape, Trudy's mother tosses her out, saying, "She's a slut." Lil Steve's mama chooses her man over him, forcing him to live in his car. Trudy's friend Vernita's salon business tanks when her protégé steals her clients. Ray Ray, Trudy's high school sweetheart, risks going back to the pen, and Charles, obsessed with Trudy, believes he deserves an affair after Flo steals the money they were saving for a house.

People do dramatic things when they're up against the wall. Some drink, some steal, some lie to their friends. Trudy taps into each character's need when she plants the seeds for a robbery. *Want Some* is a high stakes tale of revenge with a female shot-caller who may be way out of her league . . .

**Also by Pam Ward**

*Want Some Get Some*

*Bad Girls Burn Slow*

Published by Dafina Books

# Want Some

## PAM WARD

Kensington Publishing Corp.
kensingtonbooks.com

DAFINA BOOKS are published by

Kensington Publishing Corp.
119 West 40th Street
New York, NY 10018

Copyright © 2007 by Pam Ward

All rights reserved. No part of this book may be reproduced in any form or by any means without the prior written consent of the Publisher, excepting brief quotes used in reviews.

If you purchased this book without a cover, you should be aware that this book is stolen property. It was reported as "unsold and destroyed" to the Publisher and neither the Author nor the Publisher has received any payment for this "stripped book."

All Kensington Titles, Imprints, and Distributed Lines are available at special quantity discounts for bulk purchases for sales promotions, premiums, fund-raising, and educational or institutional use. Special book excerpts or customized printings can be created to fit specific needs. For details, write or phone the office of the Kensington special sales manager: Kensington Publishing Corp., 119 West 40th Street, New York, NY 10018, attn: Special Sales Department, Phone: 1-800-221-2647.

Dafina and the Dafina logo Reg. U.S. Pat. & TM Off.

ISBN-13: 978-0-7582-1776-9
ISBN-10: 0-7582-1776-5
First Kensington Mass Market Edition: June 2014

eISBN-13: 978-1-61773-040-5
eISBN-10: 1-61773-040-8
First Kensington Electronic Edition: June 2014

10  9  8  7  6  5  4  3  2  1

Printed in the United States of America

*To my supersonic daughters
Mari and Hana*

# Acknowledgments

Much gratitude to: My wonderful, sassy mother, Bonnie Moore, who drove us around in a VW bus and taught me the meaning of *family;* my unstoppable father, the architect, James Moore, who zoomed his 911 with zest (rest in peace, Daddy); my blood sisters, Linda and Lisa, whose cars died or blew up on freeways and who helped and hoorayed me in countless ways; my brother, Jimmy, whose ride always stays clean, thanks for all the raw material and always being there; Aunt Joyce and Aunt Steph, my cousin Rachel who typed this from chicken scratch, we won't say how many cars she had; to all the rest of my family, especially my sweet Grandpa George who gave up driving at 90 but still has steam in his eyes.

To Michelle Clinton and Bob Flanagan of Beyond Baroque Literary Arts Foundation; to Leonard Miropol's proofreading eyes; to Eso Won Books, the World Stage and Beyond: Wendy, Wanda, Vee, Nancy, Michael, FrancEye, Peter, El, AK, Merilene, Kamau, Watts Profits, Rafael Alvarado, SA Griffin and to Eric Priestley who peeped me some game; to Terry Wolverton and Heather Haley of the Woman's Building and to Guava Breasts: Michele Serros and Nancy

## *Acknowledgments*

Agabian; to Arvli who encouraged all my artistic endeavors, to Rob Cohen of Caffeine; to my homegirls, Alane O'Rielly, Claudia Bracho, Jeannie Berrard and Francine Lescook; to my new son, Ryan, to Michi and Ron Sweeney and the entire Abrahams family.

To my amazingly tenacious agent, Stephanie Lee, who believed in me from day one; to Selena James at Kensington and to my editor Stacey Barney who put gasoline to this dream. And lastly, to my beautiful and brilliant daughters, Mari and Hana, wear your seatbelts and roar and to *mi amor*, Guy Abrahams, an Olympian who held my hand the whole way and showed me the road to true bliss.

Want some get some,
bad enough take some!

A schoolyard threat sung before a fight.

# 1

# Flo and Charles

Some folks will do anything to get what they want. Sell their mama in a heartbeat and not miss one note. Oh, they'll smile; grin so big they show all their back molars. But don't turn your back. Shoot, you better not blink. 'Cause there's those who'll yank a bone from a starving dog's jaw, or climb a tree just to peek at the stuff in your yard.

It was May, and L.A. was a bronze deep-fried hot. The year 1997 was the worst ever heat wave on record. With all the windows gaped wide there was still no damn breeze. With his head in the freezer, Charles could not cool off. He looked at Flo's scowling face and groaned. All he wanted right now was to get out the apartment. In his mind's eye, he could already see Trudy on stage. It was the tragic way she swayed, singing with eyelids half closed, looking half sleep or strung out on dope. She was stacked. Had a break-your-neck-just-to-look kind of body. Men who'd already grabbed their car keys and stood up to pay sat back down in their seats and ordered more whiskey when Trudy came out on stage. When she sang, all the men would lean up in their seats, 'cause her hug-me-tight dresses showed off plenty of meat and sent waitresses back for more shots. Just watching her made Charles feel like he committed a crime but he took what he could like a crook.

And now he was in deep. There was no turning back. Charles stared at the intricate veins in his hand. It was dangerous but Trudy said they would go fifty-fifty. Wiping the sweat from his brow, Charles bit his own fist. He wanted it so bad that he could taste it.

Looking back, it all started with that smashed liquor bottle. Charles was coming home late, well past twelve on some nights, and Flo couldn't take it much more. She had a locksmith come over and change the locks on the doors, then she waited for Charles's car. Oh, he pounded like mad trying to get in that night. He ran to the front, then around to the back, yelling "open the door" over and over again, insanity soaking his eyes.

They lived in a backyard duplex, and the man upstairs groaned. Moving his arm under his pillow, he reached for his gun. He wanted to shoot through the floor.

During the racket, the neighbors began clicking on their lights. Some of them drifted outside in their robes trying to see what the heck was going on.

Flo didn't budge. She sat in the living room amused.

"Serves him right," she said smugly. "He can just sleep outside. That's what he gets trying to creep in this late."

But something inside Charles snapped while he pounded that door. Like a dropped glass, or the sharp blasting sound of a gun, or a bat someone swung in a car. He grabbed a giant ceramic pot, aimed it at the back door, and tossed it right through the paned glass. Charles stuck his hand in, twisted the lock, and walked through the busted pot and chunks of dirt on the floor.

Flo ran to the kitchen to survey the damage. "Are you crazy? Look at all this mess!"

"Why the fuck did you lock me out?" Charles edged toward her face. He wasn't tall but he was broad-shouldered and wide. He looked like a hotel front door.

"Because," Flo told him. "I'm sick of this, Charles! You're always coming home late. Always out at the club. What the hell is really going on?" Her anger only masked a sad, bitter wound. A hurt so deep that her bottom lip started quivering hard until she had to bite her lip with her teeth.

"You don't know shit!" Charles yanked the liquor cabinet open. He rarely drank more than an occasional beer. But during these last two fast weeks, he'd been drinking a lot. He couldn't eat. He couldn't sleep. He was butchering his job. But how could he tell Flo that? Grabbing a Jack Daniels bottle, he took a big, sloppy swig. "Stay the fuck out of my business, okay?"

"You better not be cheating." Flo's narrowed brows scolded. "If I find out, you'll live to regret it."

Charles held the throat of the fat liquor bottle. He watched Flo out of the rim of his eyes. He was seething from being locked out, and she was threatening him now! This was too much for Charles to bear. So after wielding the bottle around for one lunatic minute, he flung it against the wall, smashing it to bits, just inches away from Flo's head.

Vicious shards scattered all over the room. Glass bashed into the porcelain sink and the booze left a huge ugly stain on the wall.

Charles grabbed his keys and rushed out the door.

"Come back!" Flo screamed, her voice like a mallet. "You better clean this up. I'm not playing with you, Charles!" She chased Charles through the weeds and down the long, busted-up driveway. She chased him all the way out to the grassless front lawn. She chased him right into the middle of the trash-ridden street, her whole face a wreck with hot rage.

But Charles walked fast. He refused to look back. He hurried down the walk and jumped back in his car.

"Go ahead and go, you postal-working punk. But if you leave, I may not be here when you get back!" Flo smacked her own ass, letting her hands trace along her hips. "I know you want this, huh? You begged for it last night!" She smacked her ass again, stretching both arms toward the sky, then she licked one of her fingers and touched her behind, making a fried bacon sound with her tongue.

Charles didn't look back. He switched on the ignition. He revved it so long some of the neighbors held their ears. And when he shoved it in reverse and backed the thing out, his tires left dark marks in the driveway.

"You want me!" Flo screamed, but only his taillights noticed. Charles was already gone.

Flo and Charles played the same routine a hundred times before. Flo pretended she didn't care. She tried to act nonchalant. But she loved Charles as much as a junkie loves his drugs. Craved him like a drunk does that last sip of scotch and even in her rage, standing in that cold concrete street, she'd suck a golf ball out a water hose to keep him.

But deep down something had begun to eat

at her lately. Each day she felt something was slipping away. Oh, she laughed with her friends, pretended everything was okay. "Charles is just singing that same tune again. He'll be back," she'd say, making her voice seem upbeat, but those worry lines came just the same. Flo was thirty-four and a good twelve years older than Charles. Not many folks knew. You couldn't tell by looking. But Flo felt the age gap growing wider each day. Though she joked on the phone, she was really afraid, scared that Charles would make a play for a woman his own age.

Squeezing the steering wheel, Charles raced through the streets like a demon. He could still see Flo's smiling face in his mind. It was that cold laugh of Flo's that Charles hated most. It said he would never be anything in her eyes. It said she saw him in all of his smallness. It was that laugh he wanted to smash when he snatched that glass bottle. It was that laugh he wanted to leave, to drown out completely as his tires ate the road back to Dee's.

But wait now, we're leaping ahead of the story. There's a whole lot of mess that went down before this.

# 2

## Dee's Parlor

"Hit me again, damn it!" Tony smacked down ten dollars.

"They say money'll bring out the worst in some folks." Pearl smiled over the arch of her worn yellow cards. "Some'll kill just to get the last five from the jar."

"No one gives a hot fuck 'bout five bucks in a jar." Tony smacked his hand hard on the table again. "You gonna play cards or sit there and yap?"

Pearl ignored his remarks and munched on some pretzels. "Where's Miss Dee, huh? I ain't seen her in months. You got her hidden in some room or did you bury her in the yard?"

Tony ignored her and downed the remainder of his beer.

"I see what you're doing and I'm telling you it's ugly."

"Ain't this about a bitch. Have you looked in a mirror lately?" Tony slapped his friend Stan so hard on the back that Stan's drink sloshed all over his hand.

"You come up in the world, Tony," Pearl told him, unfazed. "Wasn't that long ago you were living hand-to-mouth on the street running a sneak game outta some fool's garage."

Tony stared at his cards and ran a hand around his stomach. He was a whale of a man, leaning on the mean side of fifty with a black, gummy smile, a bad smoker's hack, and a deep love for Johnnie Walker Black Label scotch. Tony was a pasty man who thought being fat was an asset. His conked hair was feverishly brushed to one side and held with a thick coat of Murray's grease. He ate rich food and resented having to ever work hard. If he did work, he spent more time eyeing the shapely legs going by, examining women's calves and trying to sniff at their breasts as they bent down to look through his stacks.

See, before working at Dee's Parlor, Tony sold these cheap posters. Used to lean them against the front of Dee's wall every day. The kind of bad art you see at gas station corners. Awful blurred drawings of Malcolm and King. Sadly drawn kids holding balloons in a tub in frames so damn cheap they put nicks in your hand.

"Seems like yesterday Tucker brought you into this place. It was '91, wasn't it. You wasn't but fifty and some change. In six years you're running the whole got damn club." Pearl shook her head slow, staring around the club sadly. "Hiring you was the worst thing he did before he passed."

"Tucker liked me. He hired me for my great gift for gab." Tony smacked Stan again and Stan's drink sloshed over his arm. "Hell, he told me my people skills dramatically increased the bar's tab."

"Humph." Pearl ignored him. She studied her cards.

Tony smiled, wiping the table until it gleamed. He threw the dirty rag across his broad shoulder. He poured his good friend Stan another stiff drink. Stan came to Dee's and stayed drunk every day.

"Tucker was glad he picked me. He considered me an asset." Tony nudged Stan, and Stan smiled at his glass. Agreeing with Tony meant he could drink free.

"You an ass, all right," Pearl said. "I will give you that."

Tony leaned like he wanted to take a good swing at Pearl.

"Oh, I really wish you would," Pearl said without flinching. Eventually Tony slowly sat back.

Pearl looked around the club. It had changed so much lately.

Dee's Parlor was a low-lit supper club that sat on the south side of neglect. It was on the hit-and-run corner of Washington and Tenth Avenue. Used to be an aquarium shop owned by a Chinese family, in the sixties. But after the Watts riots broke almost thirty years ago, the Chinese folks packed and left, moving to the west side to be with the whites. Washington Boulevard wasn't Watts, but it didn't matter back then. It was too close to all that black skin.

"Hit me again!" Tony barked, scratching the table with his cards.

"When Mr. Tucker bought the place it had been boarded up for years. He cleaned it, bought some used stools, tables, and chairs. Miss Dee cooked them big vats of well-seasoned food. Dee's Parlor used to be the best known black-owned restaurant in town." Pearl smiled and fanned her chest with her cards.

"What about Leo's on Crenshaw or Phillips in Leimert Park?" Tony lit a cigarette and blew the thick smoke.

"Or Johnny's Pastrami," Stan said, wiping his lip.

"And everybody knows Woody's keeps 'em lined up over on Slauson. You can smell their smoked beef from the curb." Tony rubbed his gut and smacked his lips as if he could already taste it.

"Those are small take-out shacks where folks get food in brown sacks. There's not many sit-down places to go any more. Green's shut its doors, and Memory Lane closed down. The Parisian Room is only a memory now. Shoot, Dee's Parlor is the last of the few standing."

"Why you telling me?" Tony asked. "Shoot, I was there too. You gonna play Tonk or you gonna get your photo book out? No one gives a hot fuck 'bout none of that stuff now."

But Pearl didn't care what Tony said and kept on talking. Stan didn't care either. He didn't want to talk. All he wanted was another free beer.

"Restaurant used to be a nice place you could take your lady after a date. You could catch a show or get a quick nightcap. An alligator bite went for one forty-five. A pucker shot set you back only a buck and a quarter. 'Member when well drinks were barely two dollars a glass? Shoot, a whole pitcher of draft was just one ninety-five." Pearl smiled, fanning her cards in her face. "Things were real nice back in the day."

"Back in the day's all you talk about now. Who cares what stuff used to cost way back then? Them days is gone. All I care about is how much to charge folks right now." Tony studied his cards. He scratched the side of his head and looked concerned. Stan pretended to look concerned too.

"I remember the singers. Shoot, we had the best talents! Esther Phillips sang here twice; we had Little Milton and Millie Jackson. O. C. Smith sang here so much the place was practically his home. Dee's rocked from Tuesday to four a.m. Sunday. Used to hear laughing and champagne bottles popping all the time. Oh, we had us a grand time back then." Pearl stopped and looked around; a sweet smile was on her face, but it changed looking at the rundown tables and chairs. The ugly black bars on the windows and doors made the once-bright place musty and dark. "We used to have good people. Didn't need them damn bars. Now all you hear is crashing bottles of beer and rowdy, loud, shit-talking men shooting craps."

"Shoot. We got people!" Tony stared at her hard. "Plenty of folks be lining up to come to Dee's now!"

"Different kinds of people." Pearl glanced at Stan.

"All people's the same. They all got the same wants."

"How the hell do you know what all people want?"

"I know what men want, and it's always the same." Tony held his cards with a confident air. He had a nine, a jack, and an ace. "They want money, and a good place to get a cheap drink, and some nice leg to see while they're there."

Stan nodded at Tony. Tony smiled back.

"Humph," Pearl muttered. She stared at her cards. She thought Tony was as dumb as a sack of manure. "If I had a dollar for every cockamamie thing I heard in here, I swear I'd be a damn millionaire." She stared hard at Tony over the rim of her glasses.

Tony got annoyed waiting for Pearl and sat up in his chair. "You gonna play or just sit and talk shit?"

"I dreamed about Miss Dee." Pearl smiled at her cards.

Tony squirmed in his seat. He tapped out a new Winston. He did not like this subject at all.

"She told me she doesn't feel safe anymore." Pearl held his eyes until Tony twisted in his seat.

He took a deep drag, blowing the smoke nice and slow. "Girl, please, nobody cares about your stupid-ass dreams." He didn't want to show she intimidated him one bit, so he stared straight back at her face. "Why don't you just mind your own business and play?"

But Pearl was no fool. She knew what he was doing. In these last months, Tony acted like Dee's Parlor was his. He put bars on the windows. He bought a wrought-iron door. He had the door hung with the hinges screwed on the right so the cops would have a time busting in. He started gambling and all kinds of betting on sports. He hired a strong-armed ex-boxer named Percy to stand watch and a felon who worked part-time named Ray Ray.

"I ain't dumb. You got them bars so no one barges in here—the same kind you put all over Miss Dee's house right before you carted her away. I remember. I saw Miss Dee change. She slipped down to nothing in no time at all. She's a pitiful size six if she's a day. You never feed her. She barely got out the bed. She stopped coming to the club after Mr. Tucker passed. I bet you got her holed up somewhere with the shades all pulled down. I still remember the last thing she said. She said, no matter how sunny each L.A. day blazed, to her everything turned gray. Like the whole world got old. Like some white clothes that got washed with a batch of black socks."

"I don't give a fuck 'bout no got damn black socks. Miss Dee was getting too old for this place. You got to have a man to run a hard place like this."

"This place wasn't hard until Miss Dee met you."

"She likes me." Tony grinned. "Whatchu want me to say. She had a twinkle in her eye whenever I came by." Tony held in the smoke. He let it float through his teeth. His smile was as wide as the Hollywood sign. "Don't hate the player, hate the game."

"You been eyeballin' Miss Dee like a fly does a steak. Hovering around her shoulders like a moth-eaten stole, waiting to swoop down and make your next move."

Tony drank a huge gulp and vulgarly belched. Stan took another swig too.

* * *

Truth was, the best part of Miss Dee's day was when Tony stopped by. Over the past year, she saw him at least once a day. She was never good at keeping the books at the club. She couldn't make heads or tails from the papers he shoved under her face. She'd sign them all fast to get them out of the way so she could ask Tony if he wanted some cake or a piece of See's candy, anything to make Tony stay.

And Tony kept coming. He liked telling Miss Dee lies. All of them were about someone dying. "You know, Miss Jenkins passed today. They found her dead in the tub." Tony would relish it with graphic details about flies. He liked watching the fear lodge inside Miss Dee's eyes.

All the stories about him always ended the same. He always had some financial problem. Some, "I'm so broke" woe. His car was on the blink or he had a leak in his apartment or his bum knee was messing with him again. Then he'd wait while Miss Dee wrote him a check. He made a mistake once and told the truth about Trudy. Miss Dee was so upset she wrote Trudy a big check. But Tony endorsed Trudy's check to himself. He wasn't about to let some young fool cut in on his pie. Especially that fast little tramp.

From then on, whenever Miss Dee asked Tony about Trudy, he just made up stories. "Why, she's fine, Miss Dee. Trudy's doin' real fine lately."

Tony picked up a dark, nutty piece of See's candy and plopped the whole thing on his tongue. "Why, that girl is a regular college gal now. She's up at U-C-L-A, yessirreebob." Tony licked his bottom lip, sucking off the soft chocolate. "Naw, Miss Dee," Tony assured her. "You ain't gotta worry about her. That gal's got big plans on her mind."

It was fun for him. Old folks were such cupcakes. Most of 'em never knew what the hell was going on half the time. Tony layered the frosting thick, said whatever he wanted, said whatever popped into his lopsided head.

Later that night, Tony went back over to Miss Dee's around seven. It was Monday, and the club was closed, so he had lots of time. He went in the living room and clicked the Lakers game on.

He was just about to fall asleep when the wooden porch squeaked. Tony sat quiet in his chair.

Trudy stopped by Miss Dee's to give her a nice plate for dinner. It was winter, but the heavy plate kept her hands warm. A bluish glow leaked from underneath the shade. A frayed blanket covered a knee. Trudy leaned closer and squinted both eyes.

"Miss Dee?" Trudy whispered, straining to see. "Miss Dee, is that you?"

When she placed her palm over the cold metal

knob, someone pulled the front door from her hand.

Tony's pale, balding head glowed under the moon. His heavy frame blocked Trudy's way.

"Oh . . . Tony . . ." Trudy stammered. "I didn't know you were here. I stopped to give Miss Dee some food." Trudy smiled, trying her best not to show she was startled. Her hand shook while holding the plate.

"Oh, you did? This damn late? You know old folks eat early. You shoulda called first. Miss Dee's gone to sleep." Tony's fat fist stayed gripped to the knob. He started to ease the door closed.

"Tony . . . wait!" Trudy said, putting one big leg between the door and the jamb. "I haven't seen Miss Dee in such a long time. I just want to check on her a second."

"Sorry, baby," Tony said, leaning against Trudy's leg. "Ain't nobody checking for shit." Tony smiled and sucked on his fat bottom lip. He rubbed both hands slow over the warm, brimming gut. He let his leg graze across her thigh.

Trudy moved her leg and glared Tony in the eye. "Look, all I want to do is go give her this plate." Trudy took another step. Her left foot was shaking. She could feel the hot warmth of his breath.

But Tony wasn't listening. The low porch light gleamed. The light rolled all over Trudy's firm, curvy body.

"Mercy alive," Tony said. "I'd sure love to taste some of yo' mashed potatoes and gravy." Tony ran his tongue around his top and bottom lip. "Look at you, girl. You done growed up! You got ripe in all the right places." He took a long drag, tossed the butt toward the sidewalk, then reached out and boldly squeezed Trudy's breast. He did it like it was the most natural thing on Earth. Like she was a fresh loaf of bread at the store.

Trudy lurched away and dropped the plate she was holding. It smashed the porch like a shot bird. Trudy was so shocked she stood numb and said nothing. Shame flooded her face and her anger made her rear back to slap him.

But Tony reached up and caught Trudy's hand in midair. "I wouldn't do that if I were you. I might hit you back." Tony held her arm but Trudy violently snatched it back.

Tony leaned back and smiled, admiring her frame. "Boy, I wish I had some of that hot fire on my stage."

Trudy stepped back but still held his gaze. "I'd never work for you, and don't touch me again, you freak!" Trudy glared at him like he was scum.

"Ewwwww wee! Girl, you just like your mama. Lotta hot fire running through both y'all's veins."

Trudy ignored him and angrily walked down the street.

Tony smiled from the door, licking his fingers and thumb. "That's one fine piece of tenderized meat."

Tony decided he'd have to play it safe from now on. He had been just about to leave once the Lakers game went off. Trudy's late visit had surprised him. He couldn't have folks sneaking around Miss Dee now, poppin' in whenever they wanted. So Tony got a slim cot and dragged it right in the room. He set it right next to Miss Dee's own bed and slept there each night just in case.

Folks say it was just to make sure Miss Dee left her Parlor to him. Others say Miss Dee never left Tony squat. Said he took that bar like he took everything else in life. Lord knows, some folks sure come out of the woodwork when folks get up in years. Showing up during the final months like they'd been coming around for years. Usually it's the ones who didn't so much as spit when the dying could still breathe. Visiting at the last minute, putting on a good face, hoping the half dead would leave them something in their will. But it sure was a shame the way Tony did Miss Dee.

See, Miss Dee and Mr. Tucker never had any children. She was glad to have a strong man like Tony around. She couldn't understand why a nice man like Tony wasn't attached.

"Why haven't you been married?" Miss Dee asked him once.

19

Quietly, Miss Dee was pleased Tony didn't have a woman. She was glad he didn't have to run home at all. She missed a man's gentle affection.

"Oh, I tried, but they don't make 'em like you anymore." Tony leaned real close with his crocodile smile. Shoot, Miss Dee couldn't see what a crowbar he was, that no woman in her right mind would have him.

"Well, you can't be from around here. I suspect Mississippi. You act like my people in Natchez. There aren't many people as kindhearted as you," Miss Dee said. She felt bad that her girlfriends had abandoned her so completely. She didn't know Tony was keeping them away.

Tony didn't care nothing about Miss Dee at all. All he wanted was her club and that big house she was sitting on now. Shoot, the area was already starting to change. The '92 riots were at least three years back and all the boarded-up businesses were being fixed or reclaimed. The mansions were starting to get fresh coats of paint. Tony was getting itchy. He always wanted more. He wasn't happy with small-change money. He wanted Miss Dee's house. He wanted her club. He wanted money and property and power and new things. He was sick of seeing all those late notices and bills. Tony never owned nothing. Not a car, not a home, not even a bike, and at fifty-six he was dealing with three women who all thought he was their man.

Tony had waited a long time for an opportunity like this. He'd seen Mr. Tucker fading away more and more each day, whittling down like a worn piece of wood. Like a mint in the middle of your tongue. Fact was, Tony was the one who saw him fall in that cellar. He waited a full twenty minutes before he called anybody. He checked around to see if anyone heard the thud of his body and watched while Mr. Tucker held his hand to his chest, heaving against the cold concrete floor. By the time the paramedics got there it was already over. Ol' man Tucker was gone.

Mr. Tucker was the last thing in Tony's way, and Miss Dee would be a piece of cake to do in. Tony would smile nice and real friendly while handing her legal papers to sign.

"Just sign this last one," Tony asked Miss Dee, "and I won't be bothering you no more." He handed her a pen and Miss Dee scribbled her name, and Tony quickly slipped the papers into his briefcase. Lord, it got so Tony could taste owning that club. Every time the boys would rattle the dice, his teeth would chatter with a greedy need to have it all. Have it all now! He just couldn't wait for Miss Dee to kick off. But she just lingered on so. He moved into her place but he couldn't stand it in there. The rank stench of her rotting body and wet filmy cough made him want to jump out his own skin.

So Tony started creeping in her bedroom at night, whispering into Miss Dee's ear.

"Die, Miss Dee," he'd say harsh and low. "Hurry up, Miss Dee. Go on and let go. Die, die," he told her each night.

Miss Dee woke feeling like someone was trying to grab her from the floorboards, like a black fog seeped inside her lungs.

Well, one night it damn near worked. When Tony came to check Miss Dee, she was lying stiff from stroke. She barely had a pulse and her whole left side was frozen. Her hands clutched the blanket and her chalk face was drawn. Her eyes looked like forty-watt bulbs.

Pearl called everyone she could and they gathered at Miss Dee's house. Everyone knew it was bad, but nobody could believe the hideous sores on her backside when the ambulance came and wheeled her out. Mercy alive! Giant bed sores the size of huge saucers, raw weeping wounds all blood red and rotten. Her paper skin ripped when they lifted her up and her howl was so long and so deep and so bad that folks had to suck in their breath.

Everybody looked at Tony a real long time, but he just smiled and shifted back and forth on his feet.

"Shoot, Miss Dee never did get up," Tony said low. He downed a quick drink from his silver flask and belched. He took a deep drag from his

Winston and coughed. Slowly they all looked away.

So that's how Tony got the club. Got everything in fact, the bank book, the house, the black drop-top Caddy, all that liquor they kept locked up in storage. And even though he put his name up in orange giant lights blinking TONY, everybody still called it Dee's Parlor.

Miss Dee's friends were so mad they wouldn't even walk on that side. The old men would mumble, shake their heads at the club, and some of them would rear back and spit. But Tony didn't care what those old-timers thought. Most of his new clientele were working-class folks. They were postal workers, plumbers, jackleg mechanics, sales clerks, and staffers from Kaiser Hospital off Venice. Folks who worked hard but liked having a really good time and wanted an easy place to talk shit and drink.

Pearl eyed Tony hard over the edge of her cards and then laid down an ace and a king. "I know what you're doing. Don't think I don't. I can smell when a dog's pissed on the floor."

Tony threw his losing cards down, ignoring Pearl's glaring face. "Come on, Stan. Let's get the gambling room ready upstairs."

"You know doggone well Miss Dee don't go for no gambling. I got a good mind to tell her about it myself." But Pearl knew this was futile.

She didn't know where Miss Dee was. Pearl was a big woman and wasn't afraid to speak her mind. "I've been working for the Tuckers too long to let it go downhill. Nothing but hooligans and ragamuffins coming in here now. I ought to call the police and have them search this place now."

Tony stacked up the cards. He never liked losing. "Listen," Tony said, blowing his smoke in her face, "I'ma say this one time so you won't forget." Tony took a deep drag, holding it down in his gut. "Stay the fuck out of my business. I'm warning you, hear? I don't pay your big ass to think."

"Miss Dee pays me," Pearl triumphantly said.

"Oh, really? Since when? Who signs yo' check? All you need to worry about is whether there's enough hot sauce on them wings. If you don't like it, then you can just get to steppin'. I got five other fat cooks just lickin' they chops, ready to step in and take yo' damn place."

Pearl stood up to leave but Tony blocked her way. He inhaled his Winston and held in the smoke. "Look at you standing there acting all high and mighty. I've seen ya skimmin', thinking no one's around. Seen you take cuts of meat and vegetables too, not to mention them wine bottles you been cartin' off lately in that bottomless pit satchel you call a purse." He stood there and waited but Pearl remained quiet. "Now get yo' ass outta my face."

Pearl stepped way back and let Tony pass.

What he'd said was true. She'd been skimming a bit. Nothing big. Nothing anyone would notice. Besides, she had three little grandkids to feed and her salary at the club didn't cut it. And how in hell could she tell Miss Dee about Tony, when her own arm had been in the cookie jar too. Slowly, Pearl went back to the kitchen, but not without mumbling, "I'm watching yo' ass. You ain't slick, sucker. I'm telling you Pearl's eyes is watching." She opened the freezer and slammed it back shut. She lifted a plant and peeked between a pile of plates. Her fifty-year-old eyes were always hunting for some kind of clue.

Tony smiled at the crowd growing inside Dee's doors. He didn't care what Pearl thought. He was holding all the cards. The club's atmosphere changed once he hired that girl. Her X-rated body had them coming there in droves and she sang like her whole life depended on each note. Shoot, even the old-timers who used to spit on Dee's steps were sneaking back over after their wives went to sleep to snatch a quick drink and watch Trudy sing.

# 3

## Trudy with the Booty

"Look, man, here she comes."

Two men sat huddled near a liquor store wall. Their folding chairs scraped against the brick as they stared. At three o'clock, in the sticky-clothes heat of '97, the men were already three or four beers deep.

Without letting his eyes leave the hot scene across the street, the older man placed his icy-cold beer on the ground. His age-spotted hand gripped the hook of his cane. With a dead, eaten-out face he looked two snaps from death. Only his eyes were alive.

"Hey, gal!" the old man growled, wiping beer from his chin. "Lemme taste some of yo' dumplins."

The younger man sported a big auburn perm.

"You gonna need some Vi-ag-ra, old man." He laughed in his weather-beaten face.

Trudy's thick, big-boned body strutted along the sidewalk on Bronson. It was a mean strip of squat apartments where bottlecaps and domestic brawls were as regular as junk mail. Where crackheads hung out at liquor-store corners, where whole packs of pit bulls ran wild. Trudy was one hellified bitch herself. Had to be on that block. It didn't pay to be soft. She walked bold and threw out a "don't fuck with me" look so folks would leave her alone. Trudy wasn't real attractive but she did well with what she had. And if big tits and hips were grocery mart items, then homegirl owned a whole store. She was a cinnamon woman with plenty of beef on her bones and a head full of slick, well-kept braids. By the time she was nine, she had a woman's full body. At fifteen, she was splitting the seams of her skirts. At eighteen, she spilled easily from a 42D. And now at twenty, her wet melted Popsicle smile could bring most men down to their knees.

Trudy kept walking fast. She glanced across the street. The tall auburn-haired man was Lil Steve.

"Why you walking so fast, baby? Hold up a minute." Rubbing his thighs, which were open as wide as unhinged pliers, he watched her like a hungry kid eyeing the stove. A neat stack of videotapes rested between his feet. He sold them for fifteen bucks each.

Trudy's razor eyes stayed straight. She kept stepping fast. She ignored the turkey-carving look in their eyes and kept her own glued to Dee's neon sign. When she passed the older man, he licked his wet chops and spat, "Girl, you a bitch and a half."

Suddenly, a car came screeching wildly down the street. It leaped over the curb and blocked Trudy's path. Its hood skidded inches away from her knees. Trudy lost her balance and fell hard against the wall. One of her fingernails ripped at the quick and bled.

"Hey, Trudy with the booty! I've been looking for you, girl!"

The Cutlass Supreme rattled as the man leaned from the car. "I want you to be in my movie!"

Obscenely, the man grabbed and held his own crotch. "I got something to put in your next scene." The man laughed, slapping his hand across his knee. His wide-spaced teeth looked like a loose picket fence.

Trudy steeled her body. She circled around the car.

"Ah, girl! Don't even try to be mad. You the one witcho ass all on Front Street."

"Hey Lil Steve," the man screamed. "Gimme another Trudy tape. I made the mistake of lending mine to Shawn and his ass left it out in the sun."

All the men watched Trudy as she strolled down the block.

"Mercy!" the Cutlass Supreme man said. "You're putting a hurting on us, girl."

As Trudy got closer, a woman sneered and crossed to the other side, covering her son's eyes with her hand.

Hiding her pain under sunglasses and casting an armored-car strut, Trudy wedged her way toward Dee's Parlor door. And then suddenly she stopped and stared at Lil Steve hard. A smirk crept across her thick maroon lips. It was the kind of smile you gave your boss when he caught you sneaking off early or gave a sales clerk when you tried to return something you already wore.

Lil Steve wanted to follow her to the club but he was banned from Dee's Parlor. His lids followed the roll of her hips toward the entrance.

See, three summers ago no one knew Trudy's name. It was the second summer after the '92 riots. People were starting to feel strong. Some of those burnt buildings were back. People were throwing huge bashes all over town with the last bit of riot liquor left.

Trudy couldn't wait. She was going to a Crenshaw High party! She was nervous about going but someone special would be there. She usually went to the movies during her mother's late dates. Trudy would sit in the dark watching the same show for hours, eating bon bons and Red Vines and warm popcorn in tubs. She sat, mimicking every single character's line, until her mother finally picked her back up.

But that night she wanted to go to a party. Ray Ray was meeting her there and Trudy begged her mother to take her. She took a long bath, spraying her neck with vanilla and piled her hair high on her head.

Joan watched her get ready without saying a word and then flatly told Trudy no. "Besides," her mother said, "I don't like that bucket-of-blood area, so wash off your face and go to bed."

Trudy was devastated. She'd been planning to go to that party for weeks. It was the last one before high school was over. "Please!" Trudy begged. But Joan shut her door and Trudy wept alone on her bed.

But by ten, almost all of Joan's vodka was gone and she needed to go to the store. They drove in dark silence from Seventh to Degnan. When they hit Fiftieth, she made a left turn. Her mother studied Trudy's lace dress and her piled-up hair. She looked beautiful but Joan only glared at her daughter, swearing at her for wearing all that "war paint."

Trudy's leg barely cleared the car as her mother took off. "Catch a ride back," her mother yelled at her daughter. "I'm too tired to get you tonight."

Trudy stayed by the DJ so she didn't seem alone. Her friend Vernita was supposed to come but she wasn't there yet. Suddenly she saw him, outside with a whole bunch of guys. Ray Ray was standing in a sea of white T-shirts and creased khakis. He held court; the other guys circled his broad frame. He had a deep voice and a beautiful naughty-boy smile. Ray Ray was the reason she'd come to the party. And he stopped talking as soon as he saw her.

"Hey, girl, when'd you get here?" He brilliantly smiled. He gently took her hand and led her to the balcony outside. Trudy couldn't help staring at his black flawless skin and that grin he aimed only at her. And that's when she saw him. This thin, janky-looking guy. He shot her mean, dirty looks the whole time but Ray Ray didn't notice and Trudy ignored him. All she could think of was how close Ray Ray stood. He felt good. She could smell him. She inhaled his clean male skin. When he touched her it felt like her whole insides glowed like the cool bluish ray of blacklights. When he slowly brought her close, her mouth grazed his lips. She could feel the hot need steaming under his skin. And then suddenly it was over. The blacklight glow was gone. In a flash, everything took a harsh turn for the worse. Lil Steve came up and whispered something in his ear and Ray Ray ignored her the rest of the party. In fact, she couldn't get a ride and had to take the bus home. When she got there her mother was sipping a pink drink. "Don't worry, girl, men are just vehicles, honey. Just grab hold of one with a full tank of gas and ride that damn bitch 'til it kicks."

See, Ray Ray ended up going to jail that night and Lil Steve kept sniffing, kept coming around her house. It took a long time and a lot of rides to where she worked at the mall. It took flowers and showing up every day at her door, but Lil Steve was determined. He always played to win, and after a while he broke Trudy down.

"Don't wait for Ray Ray," Lil Steve whispered in her ear. "With his record, that nigga's gettin' fifteen, at least."

Trudy tried to avoid him but he was there all the time. He was always walking her home or asking her out, begging her just like a dope fiend. One day she agreed to go see a movie. "Please," Lil Steve said. "I only want to see this with you. Look," he said, showing Trudy the stubs, "I already bought both the tickets."

But when it came time to go he made her wait in the alley. She watched Lil Steve mack the girl working the counter. The girl smiled big and let him come in for free. Lil Steve opened the back door and let Trudy creep in. They did that every single time they went to a show. But Trudy didn't mind. It was fun sharing Cokes and watching all those flicks. Trudy, who used to sit alone in those red velvet chairs, now sat in the dark with a warm arm around her shoulders. She liked how he put the popcorn right in her mouth. No, Trudy didn't mind it at all.

After the movies he took her on shoplifting sprees. Trudy would watch Lil Steve talk while his hands smuggled items. He got alarm clocks and watches and dozens of cameras, which he sold out the back of his car. He showed Trudy the fat rubber bands attached to his pajamas, which he wore underneath his loose pants. He had elaborate ways to steal all kinds of stuff, between your legs, down the back of your shirt, jewelry stuck deep in your hair. He would go in and instantly scope the whole room, ceiling cameras, stuff that didn't have sensors on, all those dumb undercovers.

Trudy was fascinated with this life. She became a quick study. She realized her wide, shapely body was an asset. Her cleavage became a deep and reliable pocket. She started to take small things too.

But Lil Steve had his eyes on a different kind of prize. He licked Trudy's neck sitting next to her in the dark. "I want you bad, girl. You know you're my heart. When you gonna gimme a taste of them yams?"

Trudy laughed and threw popcorn at Lil Steve's head. But he gently kissed her cheek and let his elbow graze her breast.

See, Lil Steve was a pro. He knew how to take

it slow. When they got home he kissed her fingers and played with her hoop earrings. His palm barely touched her bare knee.

"I know people, baby. I could make you a star. You look a helluva lot better than them chicks on the screen." He playfully stroked Trudy's braids.

At the time, it didn't seem like much. No one else had asked for it. So she gave it like somebody who gives a nice present. She lotioned it, dressed it up in beautiful fabric, dabbed a floral scent behind her neck and the back of her calves and then draped it across her clean bed. She thought it would be like all those girls in the movies as she waited for the wonderful thing to begin. But Lil Steve ripped through her body as if she were paper. He crumpled it, shoving the wrapping aside, and the sweet gift she'd saved was like knocking over a bottle that juzzled all over the floor.

The next thing she knew, it was done and wiped up. Tossed out like yesterday's trash. It was over so fast without any emotion. Lil Steve didn't say or do any of those things in the movies. But it was too late to play the scene over again. She was stuck with the ending, whether she liked it or not. So she kept giving him some, thinking this time would be different. Trudy even felt glad when he pulled out his camera. She was flattered. In her dream world she was becoming a star. She was pleased when he aimed the video recorder toward her skin. She thought Lil Steve felt exactly the same. That he wanted to remember these candy-bar moments. That he wanted to save her sprawled out on these sheets with the moon streaming straight through the wide Venetian blinds, branding her with animal stripes. She watched Lil Steve's thumb gently press the Play button. She saw the camera's red light bleeding against his front teeth. And as the slimy film rolled around the video camera's mouth, Trudy's own lips curled up and grinned.

But Lil Steve's eyes were focused on something else now. He saw Trudy's nude body as a window, a door, a new way for him to make money. He was a tall, fine, light-skinned, goateed, Iceberg Slim type who used women as easily as napkins.

"Everybody knows money and clothes make the man," Lil Steve said, smiling at himself in the rearview mirror as he drove. "A real woman knows how to keep her man happy." Lil Steve took a 'do rag from his glove compartment and patted his auburn perm down.

But Trudy found out that keeping a man happy meant buying him stuff and lending him money and letting him have sex when he asked. She wanted to drop him and asked her mother for advice. "What? Are you crazy? Fine men like him don't come every day. You're lucky he looked at you twice."

She worked at Macy's in the mall and saved

nine hundred dollars. But in three months, Lil Steve borrowed five hundred of it. In six months, her money was gone.

"Just spot me fifty," he said, kissing her cheek. "I swear I'll pay it back to you by Friday." Lil Steve always had some quick money-making scheme. "I'll double your cash, baby, you watch."

But Friday came and went and he still borrowed more. When Trudy stopped lending, Lil Steve got mad. He figured if she wouldn't lend it he'd just have to pimp her. He convinced her to do it. "I want to remember you forever." He told Trudy to lie down naked and made a movie of her in bed, and then he hawked the video shot all over town. That's how she got the name "Trudy with the booty." Everybody in the neighborhood called her that behind her back. Lil Steve said her ass had such a wide natural ledge, he could put a shotglass on it, a small bowl of pretzels, and still play a quick hand of Tonk.

It killed her to find out he was selling her nude film. Something died deep inside that she never got back. See, Trudy's life changed once that video came out. It was little things at first. Women eyeing her sideways. Or gripping their men's arms whenever she passed. She couldn't leave the house without men whistling loud or yelling lewd comments or blocking her path whenever she walked down the street. People threw things at her. They laughed when she talked. Women tossed her change when she came to the store.

"I ain't touching nothing from you," a store clerk told her once. "You're that filthy, lowdown slut from the movie."

Trudy couldn't believe Lil Steve had stabbed her in the back. Her body boiled into a pot of simmering hot greens when she confronted him outside Dee's Parlor.

"Baby, you know you got back," Lil Steve said, playing it off. "Ain't a damn thing wrong with showing off yo' stuff." Lil Steve smiled in the car mirror, continuing to comb his thin mustache. "Didn't I say you'd be famous?"

"How could you do me like that?" Trudy screamed. She was standing in the street, at the driver's side of the car. "And when are you going to pay back my money?"

"Now wait, girl, stop tripping," Lil Steve said, hanging from his car window. "Nobody never said nothing about no loan. You gave all that money to me." Lil Steve never blinked when he looked in her eyes. His face was as cold as a shovel.

Just then, a girl came out of Dee's Parlor. She was dressed in cool cream from her head to her toes. Her beige leather shoes matched her small, expensive purse. She smoothed down her dress and gently knocked on the passenger's door.

"Baby," she said in a high, whiny voice, "when are you coming back in?"

Lil Steve unlatched the passenger's side and the cream woman slinked in. She moved her small frame next to Lil Steve's thighs and his arm circled over her shoulders.

Trudy glared at Lil Steve and at the cream woman, who grinned while applying pink lipstick.

The money was one thing, the nude movie another, but seeing Lil Steve sitting with this cream-colored thing was an icepick rammed straight in her chest.

"How could you dog me like that, Lil Steve?" Trudy's whole face was ruined. Her makeup was smeared. Tears drained from her mascaraed eyes.

"Dog you!" Lil Steve laughed in Trudy's strained face. The cream girl looked back and laughed at her too. "Shoot, you the one hounding me. Following me around all the time. When's the last time I called your big ass?"

Trudy thought back and realized it was true. She'd been calling him. Been tracking him down. He was always on his way. Always telling her, "I'm coming, I'm running a little late." Trudy would wait by the giant picture window for hours. Waiting and watching the dented cars go by. Listening for his rumbling engine.

But those cold, hardcore facts just made Trudy mad. She watched Lil Steve and the smug cream-puff woman. To this day, Trudy still didn't know why she did it. She didn't want Lil Steve.

He made her sick. But she had to do something to stop feeling so bad. So Trudy grabbed the latch and yanked the cream girl right out. She got in herself and slammed the passenger's door hard. "I'm not moving," she fumed. "You can't make me go! I'm staying 'til we get this thing straight."

Trudy sat in the passenger's seat like a rock while hot tears leaked down to her lap.

Lil Steve couldn't stand watching her sit there and weep. It made him feel sad. It made him get angry. The cream girl was screaming and wiping her foot. "Look what your ghettofied bitch did to my shoe!"

Lil Steve leaned across Trudy and swung open her door. "Get out," he said flatly, with no emotion at all. He said it low like he worked in a morgue.

But Trudy was fuming. She wouldn't budge one bit. She sat on the seat like a whole mountain range. She thought of all those nasty men hassling her lately. Leering and calling her lewd vulgar names. "Fuck you," she said. "I'm not goin' nowhere. Your skinny ass can't make me leave!" She slammed her door shut and clenched her back teeth. She'd be damned if she moved one inch.

Folks were coming out of Dee's doors and circling the car, eager to watch a big show.

Lil Steve remained calm. He rose from the car slowly. Smoothing his auburn hair down, he strolled over to her side and then yanked her door handle like he was uncapping a beer. Flinging his thin arms around Trudy's thick heavy waist, Lil Steve tried to snatch Trudy out.

But Trudy was big-boned and wouldn't come easy.

"Get out!" he said loudly. He was very angry now. "You're embarrassing yourself. I don't want you no more! Can't you see I got someone else?" He pried each hand loose from the steering wheel she held and jerked her frame out from the seat.

Trudy could see the people from Dee's Parlor lining the curb three folks deep. They watched holding shot glasses and small bags of chips. There was nothing more fun than seeing other folks squabble. Tony sucked his big bottom lip and stared. The other menfolk grinned, squeezing their tall sweaty bottles. The cream girl wickedly screamed with joy, twisting her hair in her fist. Shirley, the waitress, could hardly get enough. She pushed her vicious smile toward the front and wildly popped her gum. When a hand reached to help, Shirley held their arm back.

"Don't go getting into other folks' mess," Shirley said.

It was awful to watch. Some folks turned their heads. Trudy struggled back fiercely but you could see she was lost. Suddenly there was a horrible clothes-ripping sound and the crowd tightened up at the curb.

"Stop!" Trudy shouted. She was kicking and screaming. Her red face was scratched. Her makeup was smeared. But Lil Steve had her. Had her thick juicy waist. He slammed her down hard. Tossed her there on the lawn. Laying her flat like a big sack of weeds. Trudy struggled against him. The short grass itched her back. Her dress was hiked up to her waist.

He could have fucked her right there, Lil Steve thought to himself. Shoot, he wanted to. He could feel himself getting hard. It was fun feeling her firm body squirm against his. It excited him touching all that strong, sexy flesh. Her wet agonized face made him just want to kiss her, to wipe off her tears, make her pain go away. But vanity made Lil Steve pull away. All he had left in the world was his pride. He'd die first before becoming weak. Besides, all these people were watching him now. So Lil Steve left her and never looked back. He walked inside Dee's with the cream-colored girl and ordered a tall whiskey sour.

Trudy slowly rose up, brushing the dirt from her dress. Her hair was a mess and one shoe had come off. Half a breast peeked out from her bra.

"Slut," someone mumbled.

"That's what the bitch gets."

"She's the video chick, huh?"

"Yeah, that's that heifer."

"Serves her right, being so damn fast and nasty."

The folks from Dee's Parlor started throwing out comments. The men were unconsciously stroking themselves, while the women sucked hard against their tongues.

But Trudy stayed on the ground and stared everyone down. She let out a howling melodious scream. The hate in her face made them all look away, and one by one they went back into Dee's.

Tony lingered by the door. He inched toward the curb. He leaned down and offered her his fat outstretched hand. Reluctantly, Trudy let Tony lift her back up. He cracked open a pack of Big Red cinnamon gum as Trudy adjusted her dress.

"You held that audience, gal." Tony inhaled his Winston. His eyebrows rose up as he slowly exhaled. "That yell was at least seven octaves." Tony put a warm stick of gum into Trudy's sweaty palm. "I'll give you a shot on the stage if you want."

"Yeah, right!" Trudy bitterly said, brushing dirt off her behind.

"Naw, girl, you have talent!" Tony eyed her backside. "You can sing at my club anytime you want."

Two years ago, Trudy had turned him down flat. But this time, when he flipped her a matchbook, she gingerly took it.

Tony waddled toward Dee's doors and then stopped and glanced back. His eyes rolled across Trudy's curvaceous body. "You been blessed, girl. I wouldn't waste it. Besides"—Tony lit a match in his palm and sucked the flame toward the tip of his Winston—"stage sits about three and a half feet off the ground. You can glare 'em down real good from there."

Trudy didn't shed one teardrop when she got to her house. She walked up in time to see her mother at the window, slowly closing both the drapes.

When Trudy walked through the door she could smell cooking meat. She looked at her mother with pain in her eyes. But Joan kept on ironing and spraying starch on her cotton dress. She was wearing see-through pumps and a pink satin slip. Her latte skin glowed with the friction of pressing.

Joan noticed Trudy but avoided her eyes. She didn't have time. Hall was on his way over. She kept spraying and pulling the dress with one arm. Joan kept the place spotless. The house stayed impeccably clean. Joan believed a clean house reflected who you were. She worked hard to be perfect herself. Though it was an old crafts-man home, everything in the place sparkled. The polished wood made it look rich.

Joan held down the iron. She checked the

watch on her wrist. Trudy followed her arm as it pressed the taut fabric. Her mother scowled while applying more pressure.

Joan finished the dress and pulled it off the board and wove a hanger in through the neck.

Trudy wiped her eye. A tear ran across her hand. She unwrapped the soft piece of gum.

"I don't know why you're eating that. I told you to watch your weight. You're just one plate from being obese."

This was not true, but Joan, who was built like a stick, thought that anyone beyond the trim side of a nine was just plain ol' fat, without question.

Joan walked to the mirror and started fussing with her hair. It was an enormous red wig, which she teased, hard and scratched and sprayed so much Aqua Net over the thing until the whole room filled with a dense mist. She reapplied her lipstick and doused herself with cologne. The house was a kaleidoscope of fumes.

Joan was a good-looking woman who stood over five-seven. And at forty-eight she still looked great for her age but she was the last one to know it. No, the only thing Joan saw when she looked in the mirror was crow's feet and moles and the faint hints of gray and fine lines that grew deeper each year. Though she layered on the makeup, she could not stop the clock. She was furious every time she looked in the mirror and always cursed before walking away.

"Hall's on his way, so don't mess anything up!" Joan slammed down a vase and filled it up with fake flowers. She sprayed the mahogany table with Pledge. Trudy was out of high school and Joan was annoyed with her now. She was pissed Trudy still lived in the house.

Joan feverishly rubbed the wood back and forth until it glowed. She stopped suddenly and looked dead in Trudy's eyes. "What is it? Why are you standing there staring? What the hell do you want from me, huh?"

Trudy started to say something but Joan glanced at her watch.

"Look, I need you to get me some ice from the store and pick up my stuff from the cleaners, okay?" Joan created errands to get Trudy out of the house. She gave her an endless list of things she wanted to have done and if she couldn't get rid of her that way, she dropped Trudy at the show, anything to get her out of the room. But no matter where she sent her, no matter the task, Trudy would always come back. She couldn't stand the way Hall started to look at her daughter. She saw his eyes. The way they traced her young frame. It made Joan sick to no end.

But Trudy couldn't go out now. Not after what just happened. She went in her room and closed the door.

"What did I tell you?" Joan asked, following her in. "Hall's on his way here. I told you I need some ice and I don't need you sashaying around here."

Trudy frowned, holding her pillow to her chest. Warm tears rimmed the edge of her lids.

Joan got in her face. She spoke to her slow. "I need ice," she said low. Trudy felt her hot breath. "Get up and go get it now, like I said!"

When she still didn't move, Joan popped her leg with the rag.

Trudy quickly got up. She rubbed her stung thigh. But something snapped before she reached the front door to leave. See, Trudy was eighteen and not a kid anymore. After what happened at Dee's, Trudy didn't care what happened next. And that word she held down for so many years, well, it crashed like a mug on a porcelain floor. It jumped from her throat and raced from her tongue way before she could snatch the word back.

"Bitch," Trudy said.

Yes, there the word was. It was as bold as a cherry in a clear crystal glass.

Joan dropped the rag and stared hard at her daughter. A smile passed over her red, pursed-tight lips. It was almost as if she'd been waiting for this moment. Trudy gave her a reason, an excuse to release her fury. Trudy became a place for Joan to stash all her rage.

Trudy tried to back away but Joan snatched her wrist. Joan wheeled back and whacked Trudy's face with the back of her hand. Trudy's whole head swung back and she fell against the wall. So hard in fact, Joan's own hand stung from the blow.

Joan walked from the room and fumbled through the kitchen drawer. She came back with a long wooden spoon. Joan smacked Trudy hard across her legs and her arms. She gripped the spoon's handle like it was a weapon. She covered Trudy's body with tiny welts. Trudy yelped as the wood ate her skin.

"You want some more of this, huh? Calling me out my name! You dumb, stupid, big-butt slut!"

Trudy tried to lurch away. She tried to avoid Joan's raised fist.

"I saw you in the street with your legs in the sky." Joan covered Trudy's thighs with a dozen quick smacks.

"I'm not having my man think I live with a tramp!"

Trudy tried to ward off the blows but Joan didn't stop. It felt like a million bees stinging her skin.

Joan struck her with the spoon until it snapped right in half. Joan was outdone. She had lost all control. Her anger wasn't just for Trudy but she didn't care. All she could feel was a tidal wave of rage. An anger that grew harder to manage each day. She struggled between wanting to hold Trudy tight and tossing her against the back wall. It was Hall she was furious with but she'd never admit it. It was Hall she thought of when her hands circled Trudy's throat. She only let go to answer the phone.

"Oh, hello!" Joan said quickly. "No, baby, I'm not breathless, I just came in from taking out the trash. Uh-huh. Oh, yes, you can come over late. I've got a nice roast on and a boysenberry . . . Oh, you ate. That's okay. No, I'll still be up after one." Joan kept her voice upbeat but Trudy could see the change. Hall was going to be late again.

Joan walked to the closet and grabbed a rotted-out suitcase. She threw it toward Trudy and it slammed against the bed. "Get out!" was all she said.

The next thing Trudy knew, she was out on the street. She stayed at a friend's place for a couple of days, then got a dumpy one-room unit off Western.

Trudy got clothes conscious after being kicked out by her mother. And as the video began to circulate more and more, her exterior was what mattered to her now. What she wore became important. It was her focal point now. She wanted to prove she was better than the girl in the nude movie. Trudy became hellbent on reinventing her image. Stealing was merely a means to an end. It became a game. It felt more like a sport. Each store was a quest. A victory. A challenge. It satisfied her unquenchable desire to feel special and a hot, burning quest for revenge.

In two months, her closet was jammed full of clothes. Trudy never left the house unless everything matched. She'd snatch something out of every store she ever walked into. It could be a small pair of gloves or a full-length wool coat. She stole so much and so long, it was part of her now. It was way beyond habit. It was like a disease. Clothes became her drug. She was totally addicted. Stealing satisfied an insatiable craving she had. She would glide both her hands across rack after rack. She loved touching fabric. She loved rubbing new textures. There were hundreds of colors in a variety of weights. Silk and the glorious smoothness of satin or the animal feel of cashmere.

Clothes allowed her to be completely new every day. Clothes lifted her up, above all those mean wagging tongues. Clothes became a shield from the dull poverty of her life. It made her life finally feel alive and exciting. And that wild panic she got from getting away clean almost felt better than sex.

Trudy loved stealing from the male shop owners best. The power she felt was intoxicating and intense. When she went in she felt like a strong sexual magnet. In the dressing room she would always leave the door slightly ajar. They saw her wiggling out of her skirt. Saw it fall to the floor. They watched her dangle a leopard print shoe from the end of her toe. The show she put on got those men so distracted. They were so busy watching her thick luscious hips or her jiggling cleavage that they never once looked at her hands. Trudy stole in the open. Right out in front. That's where the thrill was. That wild, crazy panic. Where her heart beat so loud her eardrums were bursting. The lunatic moment before her feet hit the door. When her blood raced and her breath sounded like a chased dog. When each foot turned to stone and the world moved in slow motion. She would try to walk natural, force herself not to run. It was maddening to breathe while her whole body screamed. Like car alarms were going off in her brain. It was hard trying to appear calm, passing stock clerks, or managers and those damn undercovers, keeping her eyes locked on the cool freedom outside, during the eternal long stroll to the door.

So in three summers Trudy's life had dramatically changed. She was no longer a lace-dressed girl, eager to go to a party. She got kicked out and took Tony's offer and started working evenings at Dee's. In no time, she was living in the fast lane herself. She met scammers and sharks and slick-talking women who came to Dee's Parlor every day.

"Hey!" Lil Steve screamed but Trudy ignored him. He wiped the sweat off from this boiling-hot day.

The men whistled loud. They made awful sucking sounds. But Trudy walked tall. She kept her head high. She climbed the two steps to Dee's wearing a plum silky sheath and four-inch-high brown snakeskin slides. Before Trudy cleared the door she smiled sweetly at Lil Steve and then disappeared behind the door.

"Shouldn'ta let that thing go," the old man told him.

I know, Lil Steve said to himself.


Trudy walked down the hall to the dressing room door and sat by the giant chipped mirror. She hid her purse underneath a big pile of clothes and changed into a long, glittering gown. Trudy sat still and stared. She sighed to herself. She glanced at the big pile of shimmering clothes. No matter how many new outfits she put on or tore off. No matter how many new looks she paraded around town. No matter how much she wanted to feel like she sparkled, inside she felt deader than lead.

There was only one time Trudy felt truly alive. One crystal moment when she shimmered within. That was just before Sonny leaned and gave her the nod. When the house lights went dim and she glowed in the strobe light. Singing on stage filled her up with a new kind of blood. It erased all the traces of her bottlecap life. She imagined herself a bright, giant star. She could rule the whole room with her drumming hip-bones. She could hypnotize them with each wiggly dip. She saw their eyes melt like ice cubes while watching her body. She could stop folks from talking. Hold them hostage with each note. Her throat, wet glossed lips and big hips were weapons. She drowned out the occasional cackles of women because their men sat there spellbound, straining to hear, glued to each sultry move. And even though most of those eyes never rose above her neckline, even though some got drunk and spilled booze on her dress, even though some of them pinched her or snatched at her body. They were reaching for her. It was her they were after. Not the gambling or liquor or the buffalo wings. All those hot thrusting hands were stretched out for her. The feeling from being on stage stayed after the house lights switched off. Long after the sounds of their glorious clapping. She became dizzy to please. She lost all inhibitions. She was determined to sharpen all their dull, worn-out lust. Like a drunk she swayed recklessly over the stage. She shook her big juicy breasts in front of their faces. With one foot near the edge it felt like she might fall. She flung out both arms, bent her neck back and roared. Because this moment, this one time she felt like she shined. Like a diamond, she felt totally see-through and free. Tony thought he was lucky getting this young chick to sing cheap. But the hot power she got from being on stage, she'd have sung in Dee's Parlor for free.

But something gnawed at her awful, like an old cat with fleas. Each day the stealing got progressively worse. Each time she took something she wanted something more. That victorious feeling would never last long. She wanted something else. Her thirst for revenge was a constant burn. She tried to stop lots of times. She knew it was wrong. But her hunger kept growing, kept itching her skin. Sometimes she'd wish she would get caught to make it stop. Sometimes she wished someone would just snatch back her hand. That someone would notice all those bags she dragged home, but nobody ever did.

# 4

## *Vernita's*

It was a mean, nasty hot in '97 during summer. A new tube of lipstick could ruin the bottom of your purse. If you wore your hair down you wanted to go have it whacked just to get that hot stuff off your back.

Flo sat in the chair as warm water filled her ears.

It felt good to finally get her hair done again. It was one of the few pleasures she had. It was a place she could go and feel right at home. Having her whole head a mess gave her a sense of abandon. The close way you sat while someone worked on your locks. The quiet dignity you kept while your hair stood on end. It was intimate. It made you all feel connected. Giving you a kitchen-chair nearness, like mother to daughter. The genuine laughter, the low, hushing tones.

The comb gliding slick or fighting through knots. The "wait now," "girl, hush" or "if I'm lyin', I'm flyin'" that rocketed across the hot room. But underneath the brush and the warm, calming water, over the robe at your throat and calm hands at your neck, there were pitchforks and ovens that could sear off your skin. Hot metal combs that could mar both your ears. Chemicals that bore through the first layer of your scalp and could singe the hair right out your nostrils. The beauty shop, the pit stop to glamour and pain. A place somewhere between holy hell and home.

Vernita's shop sat near the corner of Adams and Tenth, on a little side street called Mont Clair. Mont Clair was a warped piece of urban decay. Auto shops sat squat next to sewing machine stores or markets selling old milk or dusty piñatas and big stacks of Mexican bread. The painted brick buildings were tilting from earthquakes and the stucco walls were ugly from cracks. Film crews used that small stretch of street a whole lot because it was such a wrecked piece of neglect. But even in that miserable condition, if something wasn't nailed down, you can bet it'd be taken. Snatched before you had a chance to turn around fast, and before you figured what happened, before a cop answered the call, it'd be sold out of someone's beat-up van. People bought steel gates, pulled them across each shop entrance with padlocks hanging from chains like lots of loose teeth. But it didn't stop the stealing, only slowed the flow some. Because in the street there was always a steady flow of eyes, waiting for you to drop or misplace your keys, wondering if you left one of your car doors unlocked or your window rolled down, hoping for some kind of opening.

"You didn't hear?" Vernita whispered into Flo's lobe. Vernita put the last roller on a heavy-set lady who was now sitting under a loud, blaring dryer.

"Girl, you late. The shit happened months ago." Vernita pulled the comb through Flo's thick black hair.

"I'd believe anything about that hussy," an older lady muttered. All you saw of the woman was her swollen neck and thick legs. Her head was slung down in a rinse bowl.

"Serves her right," Shirley said, scratching her scalp with long nails. Shirley was the cocktail girl at Dee's Parlor. She was always in everybody's business. "Didn't I say she'd get what she deserves?"

"I remember like it was yesterday the night she showed at my place. Her whole face was covered in welts," Vernita said.

"You inviting trouble having that tramp at yo' house," Shirley warned. "I'da got her a map and a bus pass."

"That was awhile ago. She got her own place now." Vernita frowned. She wanted to say something back to Shirley, but she was a good paying client. So she held the curling iron a little too close to her neck.

"Watch it!" Shirley snapped as she turned around.

Vernita left Shirley and started working on Flo again.

"Poor thing, you shoulda seen her. All black and blue." Vernita pulled the comb sadly. Flo's thick hair lay flat. "Joan must have smacked her ass fifty-two times." Vernita pulled the comb again but left it too long. It sizzled when it got to Flo's ends. "Trudy couldn't even show up to work the next day. Said she got up to go but hid in the yard. Didn't want everybody to see those large, ugly welts. Gruesome skin oozing with juice."

"I bet her mama had enough. She had to throw Trudy out. Anybody can see how skanky she is. She's your friend, Vernita, so you know better than anyone else. Joan probably couldn't take all her bullshit no more." Shirley rubbed the red lipstick off her crooked front teeth. The sun showed her pitted complexion.

"Well, I heard Trudy called her mother a bitch. Now see," Shirley said, "ya'll know she was wrong."

The washbowl woman made a loud smacking sound with her tongue. "If my daughter said that she'd be lucky to still be breathing."

"But ain't that the pot calling the kettle

black," Shirley told the washbowl woman. "Both of 'em bitches, if you ask me."

With wet hair leaking over her smock, the older woman said, "I know that's right."

"Isn't Joan still shacking with some poor woman's husband?" Flo asked.

"Stole him like someone does your clothes off the line."

"And got the nerve to still put her big foot in church."

"Um um um," the older woman said, ending the exchange and laying back down in the bowl.

Vernita pressed the hot comb near Flo's neck and she flinched.

"That's no reason to beat her or toss her into the street. Trudy told me she ain't talked to her mother in months," Vernita told them. When she brought the hot comb to Flo's head once again, Flo covered her ear with her hand.

"Some women can't stand having their men near other women," Flo said low. She thought about Charles. The hair fumes upset her stomach. She wished Vernita would stop gabbing and finish.

The older woman leaned up from the washbowl again. "That Trudy ain't got nothing but hot sin in her body." The woman wore so much mascara on each of her eyes, they looked like they were lined with black flies. "My Waymond don't want to do nothing no more but creep out at night to that damned hoodlum club to hear that skanky gal sing."

"It's the same with my Joe," another woman sighed. "I caught him drooling at her in the front row one night."

"Y'all call that singing?" Shirley laughed loudly. Extending her hand, she examined her nails. "I don't care if she's Joan's daughter or not. I bet Joan got tired of Trudy sticking her ass in Hall's face. Trudy was a threat living inside Joan's house."

"Amen," the older woman said, wiping dead hair from her shoulder.

Suddenly, Trudy's Aunt Pearl rushed through the door. "Morning, everybody," Pearl said, glancing around. She was a short, husky woman with brown, flawless skin, with a smile like she just hit the Lotto. She was one of those old-time singers who'd spent time in Detroit. Told you anything you wanted to know about Motown. "Hotown," she called it. Said everybody in there was fucking. At fifty, she could sing rings around Trudy and the other girls in Dee's Parlor, and her D-cups looked damn good in sequins. Pearl showed the new girls like Trudy the ropes and made sure they weren't dealing no dirt. Nosirree, Dee's Parlor might be sliding a bit, but Pearl made damn sure it wasn't no brothel. She was a bonafide lady but not too sidity. A saucy woman who had her own stable of men who hung near her dressing room door.

"Hurry up, Vernita! I need me a touch-up. My stuff ain't layin' right no more." Pearl tossed a stuffed 99-cent-store bag on the floor. She stuck one hand in her purse and started rummaging inside. It was a great big black bag filled to the brim with Lord knows what. Her arm fumbled around until she found what she wanted. She popped a large gumball inside her jaw.

"Well, I think it's that dirty ol' man of hers," Vernita said. "She told me how Hall was nothing but hands. Trying to reach for her braids or the hem of her skirt. My uncle eyed me sideways like that from day one. Watching me, pretending to read."

"Fill me in. Who y'all talking about?" Pearl loved good gossip as much as the next. Her eyes flickered around the packed room.

"Now, Miss Pearl, you know I mean no disrespect. But Trudy and her mama, they both the same," Shirley said. "Snatch yo' man if you ain't got him chained."

Pearl looked around the room, realizing she'd walked into a storm. She eyed Shirley like she wanted to stab her right there. Trudy's mother, Joan, was her sister.

"The apple don't fall far from the tree," Shirley sneered, ripping a hangnail off with her teeth. There was nothing she liked better than stirring the pot. She showed plenty of chipped tooth when she grinned.

"Tree, my black ass. Look, y'all don't know

squat. That child's hurt. Any fool could see that." Pearl shifted farther up in her seat.

"Poor thing's been living hand-to-mouth ever since Lil Steve started this mess," Vernita said.

"Hand-to-mouth, my foot. That heifer dresses better than me," Shirley said. "And what do you mean 'child'? The girl's twenty now. Lil Steve didn't do nothing but document the shit. That video proves what kind of woman she is."

"I saw her wearing a gold Chanel suit with these ice-pick-high sandals."

"I saw that suit too. That shit wasn't cheap. I know she's not shopping at Ross."

"Must be selling her stuff on the side," someone said.

No one knew Trudy got her clothing from stealing.

Pearl shot the woman a cold eye. "She ain't selling squat."

"Maybe she's giving it away," someone else laughed.

Shirley loved the way the conversation was going. She thought it was time to toss in a lie. "I've seen her outside of Dee's with a lot of different guys sitting in dark cars for hours."

Everyone in the room started talking at once.
"See?"
"What'd I tell you?"
"Girl, you were right!"
"Anybody seen the video?"
"Uh-uh."

"Not me."

"I heard Joan found the nude tape wedged inside Mr. Hall's Bible."

"Ol' nasty freak."

"Pork chop–eating prick."

"Joan should've put a spoon to his ass," Vernita added.

Pearl stared out the window a real long time. She wished Trudy could come stay with her but Pearl lived in an apartment house for seniors and they had strict rules on who could come in. "All I know is the menfolk have been bothering Trudy bad."

"Drooling like she's something warm from the oven," Vernita added. "That video did her in. That's all I hear people talking about now, and Lord knows working for Tony don't help."

Flo was trying to sort some things in her mind. "Exactly how long has Trudy been working at Dee's now?" Charles had been there at least three times that week.

"Girl, where you been?" Vernita asked. "Trudy's been working there for months."

"I helped her get started," Pearl said. "She needed the money."

"And y'all should see how she's singing up in there." Shirley glanced quickly at Pearl. "You know I ain't lying." Shirley stood up and started dancing real raunchy, sashaying and grinding her hips. "Got all them men in there looking at her sideways. Pearl, I know you seen her. She got all them men sprung."

Pearl shot her a look, and Shirley smiled and sat down.

"And look at you," Pearl said to Shirley. "Jeans all bunched at the crotch, looking like kitty in the meat box watching that tight fabric fight."

Vernita laid the comb down and let it heat back up. She didn't like them talking about Trudy and tried to change the subject. "That fight's coming up. Anybody taking bets?"

"Bets. Ain't that about a bitch. Black folks sho' know how to waste some good money," Pearl said. "Gamblin' is just throwin' it away."

"Gone and speak the truth." The older woman liked this subject. "Buying quick picks and playing the Daily Three every day instead of letting it build up at the bank."

"Bank! Hell, I don't even have an account," Shirley said proudly. "They'll never get their hands on my money."

"What money?" Pearl asked dryly. "You're always borrowing from me."

"I deposit mine each week. I don't play with mine, honey, and I got something if someone wants to act funny." The old woman patted what looked like a gun in her purse, then she smugly sat back in her chair.

Pearl stared at Shirley. "Some'll walk over a dollar to pick up a dime."

Vernita saw a customer coming. She went to the window to wave, but the woman raced into the shop down the street.

"And some rob you before you ever see 'em coming," Vernita said flatly.

Pearl let the gumball roll against her tongue. "And leave you to bleed in the street."

"That's what Trudy did me," Shirley snapped back fast. "That bitch stole the best man I ever had." The nail file she held gritted across her rough tips.

"Your man? You wouldn't know a man if his teeth bit your rump. Only man I seen you with left you sitting at the curb with a window cracked down, breathing on the glass like a dumb smashed-faced dog." Pearl grabbed a bra strap and hiked up both breasts. "If you gonna tell it, then get the shit right!"

"Trudy's just getting what she finally deserves," Shirley said.

"Nobody deserves the hand she got dealt." Pearl's eyes got as tight as two steak knives.

"Lil Steve started this mess," Pearl told the room again.

"Choosing the wrong man can lead you astray," the older woman said.

"Well, all I know is"—Vernita finished Flo's hair and spun her toward the giant mirror on the wall—"Trudy's a hundred percent Scorpio. Homegirl don't play. It might be today, it might be next week. You fuck her over, she don't forget. One day she'll pay yo' ass back."

Flo didn't say she was a Scorpio too. She didn't know Trudy well, but Flo did know one thing. Men beamed whenever Trudy's young frame came around. She had caught Charles eyeing her at the gas station one night. Trudy looked like the kind of woman who could have any man she wanted. At thirty-four, Flo had been around the block a few times. She watched young women like Trudy out the side of her eye.

Shirley popped her gum and grinned at the room. "Well, I'm sorry. But I don't feel sorry for that girl. Trudy's gonna get it one day, wanna bet?" Shirley pointed the nail file tip at the door. "Game recognizes game. She ain't fooling me. I work with her. I've been watching her lately. I got a good feeling she's got something cooking up her sleeve, and believe me, it ain't on the same side as right."

"You ain't been on the right side in years." Pearl gave her a harsh, deadly stare.

"Hey, Flo," Vernita yelled, quickly changing the subject. "You still breastfeeding that fine younger man?"

Flo's eyes darted around the shop. She hated discussing age. But she gave a fake laugh and began fanning her face. "That man is making me crazy."

"Don't downplay it, Miss Flo, you know

Charles is fine." Vernita was glad Flo had her a nice younger man. "He's quarterback wide and got a flat six-pack stomach."

"And gives skull like a pro, once I showed his ass how." Flo whispered that last part. She didn't want that on blast.

Vernita smiled, letting her hand rub across her round head. She was a very light-skinned woman with razor-short hair. Her green eyes gleamed in the sun. "I know exactly what you mean," Vernita whispered back.

"Hold up!" Pearl said, happy to finally change the subject. She scooted all the way up in her chair. Vernita had half of Pearl's hair perfectly curled on one side, and the other was sticking straight out. At fifty, she easily looked ten years younger and her body was as strong as a vault. "Y'all can keep them chicks; give me a rooster. Give me an older skilled man working over my back and, Lord, girl, I turn right into butter." Pearl practically rolled from the beauty shop chair. "Somebody better come mop me up."

Flo faintly smiled and fanned herself in her seat.

"Miss Pearl, you ol' hussy," Shirley said, smiling.

"Ain't no freak like an ol' freak," Vernita said, approving. She liked Miss Pearl. She always spoke frank. Real women like her were rare.

"If a man goes down south, pleases my Mississippi, I'd pop his big gun for free." Pearl smacked her own thigh.

Shirley and Flo laughed; even the washbowl woman chuckled.

"And I'd freak his ass in fifty-two ways if he knew what to do when he got there," Vernita said, snapping her fingers, waving her arm in one large arc.

"But y'all better use a jimmy. Mama don't play," Pearl said, wiping the front of her smock. "I'm done with them urine cups and trips to the clinic. Y'all keep that stuff if you want."

Flo dabbed the warm sweat welling out from her temples. She picked up a magazine and threw it back down. She did not want to talk about sex.

"Y'all laughing now but wait 'till you got a screaming brat on your back. Tell me about what feels good then!" Pearl looked at Shirley in the beauty shop mirror.

Shirley had five babies from four different guys. She sure wasn't the sharpest knife in the drawer.

"Tell him, 'no glove, no love.' Have that jimmy hat ready. Cuz I done known plenty of men in my life, but I don't know any women— once a man gets it—had any luck getting him to take it back out," she said, laughing.

"Amen," the older woman echoed.

Suddenly, the room got front church pew

quiet. Flo nudged Vernita real quick in the arm as Joan strolled in the shop door.

There was only one woman who could turn a loud, rowdy shop into a Catholic church service. That was Trudy's holier-than-thou mother, Joan.

Joan was the kind of woman who rarely smiled. When she did, it was with a half-curled-up lip that quivered like she couldn't quite hold it. She never laughed big or showed any teeth. And if she did it was only at someone else's expense. She was younger than Pearl but her face was more lined. She was the kind of light-skinned woman who felt better than most women. She spoke low, carefully enunciating each word, and walked stiff like a pool stick ran straight up the back of her dress. Although she wore a red wig, she came for the same press and curl, for the same tidy bun she'd been wearing over twenty-two years.

Flo watched Joan pick a nonexistent piece of lint from her over-starched collar. At five-seven and in heels, she easily towered over them. Acting all high and mighty with her light eyes and pasty loose skin. Joan was always talking about the good hair and keen features that ran in her family, like anybody gave a hot damn. Shoot, her hair couldn't be that good, Flo thought to herself, if she was getting it done like everyone else.

"Hello, everyone. Hi, Pearl," she coolly said. Joan took a napkin from her purse and wiped the chair before sitting down. Carefully applying some lotion to her manicured hands, she said, "Vernita, I need a full set today."

Vernita left Pearl's head to hand Joan a magazine. She got the foot pan, rinsed it in hot soapy water and plugged it in next to Joan's legs.

"That bitch makes me sick," Vernita whispered to Flo.

Flo ducked her head in a magazine and sat quietly.

"Joan ain't nothing but a white-looking snob," Shirley whispered to Flo so Pearl couldn't hear. "Whole damn family ain't nothing but crooks. Everybody knows she stole Mr. Hall from his sick wife's back door. And he charges too damn much at his store."

"You know," Vernita whispered back, bending down, "the real reason she threw Trudy out was because she was jealous. Didn't want no daughter looking better than her." Vernita dropped her comb and let that sink in.

Everybody in the neighborhood talked about Trudy and Joan. Joan did this or Trudy did that. The fine clothes Trudy wore, the Mercedes Joan drove. And even though the Benz was old and smashed on one side and their house was down the street from the rowdy Dee's Parlor, it still was the best-looking one on the block.

Joan was holding a video case in her hand. "Look at this!" Joan waved the tape all around. "Can you believe they're still selling this crap out on the street? My God, could my life get worse?"

They all stood around Joan's thin, narrow hips.

"Is that the video?"

"How'd you get a copy?"

"She ruined my life," Joan told anyone who'd listen.

"Oh, I don't think . . ." Pearl tried to stifle her sister. Joan could be so damn dramatic.

Everyone gathered tightly around the TV to see. They'd all heard about Trudy's nude movie but none of them had seen it up close.

"Girl, don't show them that!" Pearl tried to turn the set off.

"Pearl, I'm talking. Please don't interrupt. Mama taught you better than that." Joan pushed the tape inside the VCR. "Now, I'm not some dumb turnip dropped from the truck. There is absolutely no way to make a picture this close, a video this clear, without you having to know. Look at it! Sitting right there in the air. All that black nakedness hanging for the whole world to see."

Everyone stared close. Even Vernita peered in. The movie showed a young woman rolling around naked in bed.

"She posed for it. Look at her dry humping that bed!" Joan got so close, the set touched her nose. "Look at those overgrown breasts and that awful behind rising." Joan snatched out the tape and carefully sat down. "I tell you it's just plain dis-gusting!"

To Joan, a behind standing high was plain vile. She didn't understand why black women stuck their butts out like that. They should hide it, or drape it with long flowing fabric. Or walk like her own mother had taught her to do—with her hips jutting forward and her behind tucked back in.

"And her hair? Just as nappy as can be!" Joan sucked her teeth and shook her head back and forth, like Trudy's natural hair was a sin. "It's a shame the poor girl looks like her father. She didn't get anything from me."

Pearl stared amazed at her younger sister but decided to hold her tongue.

The other women didn't know what to say. Joan made them feel small. She was so knowledgeable, so dignified; she looked so damn rich. She didn't have a pot to piss in or a window to throw it out but you'd never know it by the elaborate way she dressed. She stared at the other women, flipping her long red wig hair. See, this was the nineties. The sixties were long gone. All that black pride had turned into perms, fades and weaves. Extensions were the only rage now.

Joan yanked the tape from the black cassette holder.

"She's my daughter, so I can say whatever I want." Joan pinched her nose and clenched her china-cabinet dentures.

"She's a slut. She's a big lying bitch. Turned out to be just like her father. Didn't get any of my family's genes." Joan flipped her fake hair and looked at her sister, daring Pearl to comment. She picked up an *Essence* magazine and eyed the dark-skinned woman on the front cover. "Nobody that dark should wear white."

Flo stared at herself in the mirror a long time. Her body wasn't that different from Trudy's. They were about the same size, had the same drenched-maple skin; Joan easily could have been talking about her. Flo rushed from the shop and raced down the street. All the hair-burning fumes were making her sick. She was glad to get out of there today.

# 5

## *Vernita and Trudy*

Trudy waited in her car until the last person left Vernita's shop. She watched Vernita click the lights, twist the deadbolt and pull back the grate until it latched.

"Vernita!" Trudy whispered once she got near her window.

Vernita jumped and her purse slammed against a shop door.

"Damn, girl, you scared me. What are you doing here? I know none your braids have fallen a loose 'cause I tightened you up good myself." Vernita leaned in and examined Trudy's brown scalp.

"Get in," Trudy said. "I need to talk to you a minute."

Trudy opened the passenger's side and Vernita glided right in. She handed her a heavy paper bag.

"What's this?" Vernita asked, peering inside. "Ah, girl, you sho' know what a working girl likes." Vernita pulled a pink wine cooler out from the bag. Twisting off the top, she took a deep, thirsty swig.

"Damn, girl, it's hot. I been doing heads all day." Vernita placed the cold bottle against her forehead.

"So did you talk to Lil Steve? Did he take the bait?"

"Girl, please," Vernita said. "Mommie knows how to talk to a man. That boy took the bait and ran with it, chile. He and Ray Ray been whispering all day."

A girl with a cute, sassy bob pulled up across the street. When Vernita saw the girl, her expression completely changed. And even as she downed two more large gulps, her eyes never left the car's dash.

"That's that Keesha girl I was telling you about." Vernita watched Keesha get out of her brand-new black Nissan. "Trained her myself. Taught her all my hair tricks. Now the bitch up and got her own shop."

Keesha's shop was half a block from Vernita's. Vernita's business had slumped as soon as it opened. Even her regulars were starting to peek in on Keesha, and all the new business went there without fail.

"She got lots of exotic plants and them red chairs I wanted and wood cabinets that go from the ceiling to the floor." When Vernita downed the rest of her cooler, Trudy handed her another one from the bag.

"She's been stealing my customers. Takin' 'em all, one by one. Last month I had to go into my stash to make rent, and this month is fifty times worse."

"Nobody does hair as good as you, girl." Trudy tried to cheer her friend up. She saw the pain in her eyes.

"I swear no one out here is loyal no more. I really helped that girl. Taught her everything I knew, and this is my fucking thanks."

They watched Keesha lock the gleaming black car.

"I oughtta key her new shit now." Vernita opened Trudy's door.

"Don't be stupid, Vernita!" Trudy held her friend's arm. "You know that won't solve nothing. Don't stoop down to her level. Besides, I think I can help." Trudy looked straight in her eyes.

"How?" Vernita asked, staring back.

Trudy took a wine cooler from the bag and drank half.

"'Member what we did working the hash line in high school?"

"Hell yeah, I remember. How could I forget? Both our arms hung heavy at the end of the day from all that money we stuck up our sleeves."

"'Member that ol' white lady that worked with us too? She loved your ass. You couldn't do no wrong."

Vernita smiled and added more gloss to her lips. "She was sweet. Just a little ol' grandmommie type. I stole steady next to her every day."

"She was sweet 'cause her lily ass thought you was white."

"She did not!"

"Yes she did. All of 'em thought that. 'Cause when everyone got caught and they asked us all those questions, they interviewed everyone except you."

"'Cause I was good. Color had nothing to do with it."

"Good my black ass," Trudy shot back. "Them white folks thought you was one of them is what it was."

"Well, I can't help what stupid white folks think."

"And you never said different. You sat there all quiet."

"Well, what was I supposed to do, huh? Scream in their face, 'Hey, y'all forgot one. Come over here. I want you to question me too?' Shoot, just 'cause their lily-white asses were dumb didn't mean I had to be."

Trudy always noticed how people treated Vernita. Her skin tone made folks treat her less harsh. Like they were glad to have her around. Vernita's hair was real long and feathered back then. Trudy never understood why she'd cut it off.

"All I want you to do is what you did then."

"What?" Vernita asked with her piercing light eyes.

"I just want you to play white."

Vernita's eyebrows rose up. She lowered the bottle to her lap. "A white girl. What, you're asking me to pass? You want me to play an ofay?"

Trudy knew that Vernita felt this was a personal insult. Although she was as light as most white folks come, she never considered herself anything but black.

"Why I gotta play white for your big plan to work?"

"'Cause a white girl in a bank does not look suspicious. White girls got privileges us dark sisters don't. They can walk anyplace and no one ever thinks twice. People don't follow them in stores like they're gonna take something. White girls got it easy. No one suspects them. They're like American Express. They just glide through the system and nobody ever thinks twice." Trudy pulled a blond wig and a beautiful white linen suit from out the back seat. "Just put this on. No one will ever know you're there. All I want you to do is be a decoy."

"I thought all you wanted was to get Lil Steve. Pay his ass back for dogging you so bad. Now you want me to be a damn white decoy too."

"I do, but I been thinking about it, Vernita. We can dog him and get paid ourselves."

"'We'? I ain't down for robbing no banks. Y'all can be a fool by yourself."

"I'm not asking you to rob the damn bank, Vernita. You said yourself you wanted to redo your shop. Come on, girl, I need your help."

"So me helping means I have to act like I'm white."

Trudy smiled at her friend. "Well, I sure can't do it." Trudy stroked her dark skin and fingered her long braids.

"Get some Porcelana, hell. Rub that fade cream shit on," Vernita said sarcastically.

"Yeah, that's right." Trudy downed a swig herself. "I'll turn white when pigs fly."

"Well, hell, look at Michael. Homeboy had his shit dyed."

"And I'll look like I'm going to a Halloween party. Look, you did it in high school. How is this any different?" Trudy stared down the litter-strewn street.

"I wasn't doing *it* in high school! I can't help what fools think. And I damn sure wasn't robbin' no banks. We just took a few bucks from the hash line, my God!" Vernita stared at her friend. Trudy had changed a lot lately. "You got cocky ever since you started working at Dee's. Them drunks and small-time thieves got you thinking like them."

"Just help me, Vernita. I gotta leave this place. I'm staying in that backyard unit near Western. It took me five weeks to get the place clean."

Vernita had seen Trudy's place. All the walls were rotten. The pipes leaked and someone had burned a hole in the floor. Lots of hard-looking people lived next door. She looked at Trudy's strained face. "Girl, don't be dumb. Just call her and tell your mother you want to come home. I'm sure y'all can work this thing out."

Trudy stared at all the trash leading to the liquor store door. A man stopped near their car and leaned toward her window. He licked his lips slow before speaking.

"Hey, movie girl," he said, grabbing between his legs. "I think I got what you need. Let me get a whiffa yo' stuff!"

"Step the fuck off," Trudy yelled sharply, "or you're gonna need to get some new teeth."

"Bitches!" The man spat, walking away fast.

"I can't stand it here anymore. It's getting worse and worse. I can't go anywhere without someone saying something or grabbing me or throwing things at me. And the women are as horrible as the men."

"Ignore them. Or do what you just did, tell 'em to step the fuck off."

"I do, but it's hard." Trudy's eyes filled with tears. "They're vicious, Vernita, the comments are much worse. That movie Lil Steve did really ruined my life. If I could take five minutes back, I swear, it would be that. I can't stand to walk down the street anymore. I got to do this job so I can get the hell out."

Vernita stared at her friend. She really wanted to help Trudy. She knew everything she said was true. She'd heard those cruel comments first-hand. But hitting a bank was no god damn joke.

"This ain't high school. This is a fuckin' bank you're talking. Cameras be everywhere. Even in the bathrooms. This ain't like taking nickels and quarters from school," she said.

"Look, I've already thought this thing through. We don't have to touch any of the money. Lil Steve does the work for us. He handles the drama. All you do is play decoy and leave."

Keesha must have forgotten something, because she ran from her beauty shop and out to her Nissan again. Her silver rims sparkled in the streetlight.

Vernita looked seriously back at her friend. "All you want me to do is walk in. That's all?"

"I'm telling you that's it. No sweat, I promise."

"I don't want to get caught." Vernita stared dead into her eyes.

"Being caught is not even an option, Vernita. See, we're not the ones who'll be doing the crime. That punk who fucked up my life, that's his god damn job. Not getting caught is Lil Steve's problem. You and me are going to be fine."

# 6

## Ray and Lil Steve

"Wake up, you homeless muthafucker!" Tony screamed loud. He was banging on Lil Steve's fender. It was nine o'clock at night and the streetlights were on. A slight mist had fallen on the lawn.

Lil Steve was sound asleep in the backseat of his car. The pounding sound made him bump his head against the door. He saw Tony's sour face pressed against the window. He knew what Tony wanted, but Lil Steve remained calm. As his head throbbed, he reached over and put his Ray-Bans back on. Then he slowly rolled the window halfway down.

"If you give me two weeks, I'll pay it all back with interest."

Tony smiled at Lil Steve. He took a pack of

cigarettes from his pocket. "If ifs were fifths, we'd all be drunk. Now pay up and don't give me no lip." He wasn't about to be intimidated by this dumb stupid punk whose dick just got big last week.

Lil Steve pulled up his pants leg and peeled down his sock, taking a C-note out from his ankle.

Tony stared at the bill like it was nothing. "You 'bout four yards short." Tony lit his match, sucking his lips hard against his Winston.

"I'ma have it by Friday," Lil Steve told him coldly.

"You better have, Junior." Tony's gummy grin was broad. He dropped his lit match on the front seat of the car. It made a tiny burn mark on the oily green vinyl. "If you don't, you gonna need to get a new home." Tony grabbed the money and walked to Johnny's Pastrami. He ordered three pastramis, two fries and a Coke before laboriously getting back in his Caddy. Lil Steve leaned forward, watching him close out of his clean sideview mirrors. He rolled down the window, grabbed the parking ticket from under the wiper, balled it up and tossed it out toward the gutter.

"Yeah, get yo' fat ass back in yo' ride." Lil Steve took another hundred from under the car mat and jammed it inside his sock. He got out of his car and wiped the chrome of his Impala. He folded the rag and put it back in the trunk. The car might be old and nicked on one fender, but Lil Steve kept his ride clean.

Lil Steve sprayed Armor All on the burn mark and flicked the match out. "Muthafucka," he said under his breath.

In the criminal world there were all kinds of types. Gangsters, straight thugs who would murder your mama and not shed one drop. Ballers who pulled up in white, gleaming Bimmers to hand out their small rocks to sell. Players and pimps who liked dealing women and hid in a shroud of giant permed hair with fat gold chains waxing their necks. Hustlers were the ones you got free cable from. Sold those black bootleg boxes at a hundred a pop. Or maybe they worked for the phone company once or some video shop and walked home with a bag full of tools or a catalog of CDs and movies. They did insurance fraud, real estate and credit card scams. They might carry guns, but they weren't your murdering type. Just had heat if some shit broke off raw.

See, Lil Steve was one of these. A confidence man. The kind you got to do the talking. He'd only been to juvie on a credit card scam. He walked and talked fast. Always thought he was smarter. His young-looking face lived on a stack of fake ID's. He prided himself on never getting caught. Never went to the pen once. You could tell by the crazy way he talked.

"Chili dog, chili dog!" Lil Steve screamed to

Ray Ray. He walked the short blocks to Dee's Parlor.

Ray Ray was standing outside against the wall. He had just been hired as a bouncer.

"What's hap'nin, man?" Ray Ray smiled back.

Big Percy grinned too, giving Lil Steve a pound.

"Walk with me a minute," Lil Steve whispered to Ray Ray. He threw a quick glance at Big Percy's back. "Nosy brother always trying to co-sign."

Ray Ray's black leather jacket blew in the night breeze. Lil Steve stopped when they got out of earshot.

"Every word I tol' you is the got damn truth, man. This dude is like clockwork. Every Friday at three o'clock he strolls in the bank with his double-breasted suit and puts in twenty-five grand. Blam! Just like that." Lil Steve popped his fingers into Ray Ray's burnt face. He took out a Kool and lit up the end. The match glowed against his baby-smooth skin. "But at the end of the month he takes the whole hundred out." Lil Steve pulled the tab on a Colt 45. He kept the can inside the brown paper bag.

"All we got to do is follow the dude and jack his ass on the ride home. Simple as that. Easy money, homie. That's fifty G's apiece in our pockets." Lil Steve took a swig from the bag. He passed it to Ray Ray to sip.

Ray Ray waved the can away. He leaned against

the wall. He stayed icy cool, but everyone knew he was crazy. He'd already done time for battery and assault and the word was still out on the boy in a coma. If the parents unplugged him and the little kid died, they could still charge Ray Ray with murder. That's the kind of dude Ray Ray was. Straight thug. Strong-arm man. Half Panamanian, ex-heroin addict, and you'd better watch out when his temper flared up 'cause there was no telling what he might do with a knife.

Ray Ray's narrowed eyes sliced into Lil Steve's face. Homeboy always came up with these crazy-ass schemes. Nigga talked more shit than anybody he knew, but they'd been best friends since fourth grade.

"Who told you about the suit, dog?" Ray Ray asked casually.

"Vernita hooked me up. Her girl Trudy works there." Lil Steve took another swig from the can and looked down. He never looked Ray Ray in the eye when Trudy's name came up. "Homechick still got the best ass on the block!"

"Shouldn't have let that one go," Ray Ray said matter of factly. Ray Ray had learned early to keep his emotions in check. No one knew how he really felt about Trudy. Like a cellblock, he looked colder than concrete.

"Man, I know," Lil Steve said, wiping his mouth. "I done had plenty but Trudy was the best. That girl had a whole lot of heart."

They both stopped and watched a woman walk down the street. She balanced a fat grocery bag on her hip. Her thin skirt swirled around her large calves.

"A bitch'll flip the switch once she knows yo' ass is sprung," Ray Ray said, flicking his ash. "No point going out like some punk." He said that last part more to himself. Jail had given Ray Ray a long time to think. "So, y'all still hang?" Ray Ray asked casually.

Lil Steve looked at the trash cans lining the street. "I had to cut her loose, dog. My shit was all fucked up. That's when I owed Tony that money."

Ray Ray remembered. Word was, he still owed him some.

"Man, how'd you get her to make that nude movie?" Ray Ray knew lots of women who did lots of freaky shit, but never in front of a camera.

"Had forty copies made the same day," Lil Steve bragged.

Ray Ray had one too but he never did watch it.

"Nigga, how you even think of some crazy shit like that?" Ray Ray put half a smoked joint in his mouth.

"Common sense, loc. Marketing is all. I told her I was gonna make that big ass a star. I said Hollywood's not ready for the body she got. Man, her shit looked way better than them babies in Playboy. I couldn't believe how easy they sold. All the barber shops wanted 'em, auto mechanics, men hanging at the car wash were asking for some and them dudes sitting up high at the track. I even rocked 'em at a few of my friends' bachelor parties." Lil Steve stopped to laugh at his own crazy antics. "Never had a problem having cash after that."

"You was flowin' for a hot minute, player." Ray Ray nodded. He blew his smoke out real slow.

"I sho' didn't expect her to find out, though, dog."

"I'm surprised she's even speaking to yo' ol' janky ass." Ray Ray took another long drag. "How you know this bank shit ain't her getting you back?"

"'Cause she's sprung. That's a damn woman for yo' ass. You dog 'em real bad and they still call you back. Trudy ran the thing down to Vernita the other day. Told me somebody could make some quick money off that white boy. Said they better move soon before the deal dries up. Said the tan-suit man's been talking about leaving that bank. I'm telling you, fool! We could make a killing putting that cash on the fight." Lil Steve wiped his mouth with his sleeve. "So, whatchu say, homie? You in or you ain't?" Lil Steve leaned closer into Ray Ray's marred face.

"I'm thinking about it, man."

Ray Ray was fresh from the pen and didn't want to go back. He looked down at the long silvery scar on his arm from the last time.

"Study long, study wrong," Lil Steve shot back. "Look, this Friday is the day. That gives us just enough time to place our bet and bust Tony's fat ass for good. You know he be treating you wrong at the club. Messing around with your scrilla and shit. Talking about hold your check till next week. You know that ain't right. Got all kinda money coming in every day and he talkin' 'bout hold your damn check."

Lil Steve took the forty out of the bag. He downed the rest of the can, wiping the corner of his mouth, and let it roll down to the curb.

Ray Ray stared Lil Steve straight in the eye.

"Straight up, man, is this shit legit or what? You ain't in it just to bust that big ass again, is ya? How I know you the one who ain't sprung?"

"Me sprung? Nigga, please. You must be sick. You know every woman I hit turns into an addict. She just wants my black juicy dick."

Ray Ray studied Lil Steve's smooth face. He knew Trudy wanted something. But he didn't know what. "So how's this shit s'posed to work?"

"Damn man, I done tol' you twice! Dude comes in and takes out the cash. Been taking it out every fuckin' month. All we got to do is gank his ass and go. No guns, no drama, no bullshit, all right? Man, I'm trying to tell you it's cool."

Ray Ray knew it had to be cool. He had just come back from doing eighteen months in Norco. If this went bad he could face eight years upstate. Ray Ray picked up a bottle and threw it out in the street. It crashed next to an old Dodge.

"I need to get my hands on some ends, fast," Ray Ray said. "Tony don't pay on time at the club, and things getting worse around the house." Ray Ray worked at Dee's Parlor as a bouncer. It was the only job he could get as a felon.

"Your moms don't sew at that factory no more?" Lil Steve asked.

Ray Ray fingered the cross at his throat. He re-lit a Newport and sucked the dank smoke, blowing it out long and slow.

"When I was locked up she worked late at the shop. Used to have to leave my little niece Kelly alone. So this social worker comes nosing around, asking questions and shit. Kelly lied. Told the lady Mama went to the store. You can't tell those welfare folks you got a gig, no matter how below minimum wage it is."

"Dig it," Lil Steve said, cleaning his shades.

"So the lady say, 'You here all alone by yo' self?' Man, you seen them Section Eight wenches with they wide, bulging eyes, tapping they clipboards and shit."

"Running up in here like some roaches," Lil Steve said.

"So the bitch hauls Kelly off to a foster care ward. Said Mama's unfit. Some endangerment law. Man, my moms ain't been the same since."

Ray Ray threw a rock at a parked beat-up car. It ricocheted off of the curb.

"I was locked down and couldn't do a mutha-fuckin' thing. All she does, dog, is just sit in her chair in a big apron, staring. Looking out at the busted-up pavement outside, blinking at nothing but the hot sun."

"Damn, man," Lil Steve said. That's not what he heard. He heard Ray Ray's mama was smoked out on Sherm.

"When I finally got out, I tried to watch her myself. Bought food, cleaned up the place some. Tried my best to cheer her back up. But, man, it's no use. I can't leave her alone. Almost torched the place once when she fell asleep with the stove on." Ray Ray rubbed the large burn on the side of his face. "I gotta pull all the knobs off the oven when I go." Ray Ray popped open his Newports and pulled out one more smoke.

"Look at this." Ray Ray pulled up his sleeve, revealing large, pumped-up arms. The kind you only see on wrestling shows, or on men who just got out the pen. Ray Ray lit his cigarette and held in the smoke.

"Man, I tried to go legit, but every interview's the same. Muthafuckas always asking, 'What skills do you have? Where have you worked?' I want to leap across the desk and slap the smirk from they mugs. Punks always asking questions. What can you do, what have you done? White boys don't want you to learn no new shit. They got all the fuckin' power. Own every got damn thing and do the hiring too. My parole officer told me to go work for Roadway. I don't want to sit in no funky-ass truck. Riding all damn day in a jail cell cab. Getting hemorrhoids and shit, breathing cheap gas and fumes, just to bring home minimum wage."

"That's right," Lil Steve added. "That's what I'm talkin' 'bout, dog!"

"Chump change once they gank you for taxes. Look, man," Ray Ray said, showing the inside of his arm. "I've been selling my own blood to get me some cash."

Lil Steve studied the bruises of Ray Ray's thick arm.

"They stab a long needle deep down in my veins. Make me lay down and give me cups of grape juice to drink while I watch my blood fall in a jar. I get $15 a pop each time I strap down. When I ain't manning the front door at Dee's Parlor, dog, I'm feeding Mama on plasma donations alone."

Lil Steve didn't know if homeboy sold blood or not. But he did know Ray Ray used to like him some heroin. "Listen, G, if we do this, you gotta be straight. You can't be fuckin' with no needles and shit." Lil Steve didn't want to do no heist with no addict.

"Well yo' ass can't be up on that cheap liquid crack." Ray Ray looked at Lil Steve's empty malt liquor can. But he smiled at him too. The deal sounded smooth. A little too smooth. But he had to admit, Lil Steve was one of the best hustlers he knew. Ain't been caught on no serious shit yet.

Lil Steve squinted his eyes at him hard. "So what you say, nigga? Is you down or what?"

"Yeah, man, I'm down. Handle yo' business. Meet me at the club and let's work this shit out. But listen, cuz, don't fool around and fuck this shit up. I ain't playing with yo' crazy ass. Call ol' girl and pick her brain about this mess."

"You ain't got to tell me. See, I'm Teflon, baby! Nothing sticks to me." Lil Steve flashed Ray Ray a big gold-tooth smile. "Woowee," he said, wild. "We gonna jack his ass and be counting fifties on the freeway, baby!" He gave Ray Ray a pound and did a little backyard boogie dance.

Ray Ray flashed him back a mild smile. "You's one crazy fool." He took one final drag and dropped the butt to the ground, smashing it out with his toe.

# 7

## Joan and Pearl

Pearl poured her sister Joan a shot glass of tequila. Two frosty margaritas sat next to each short glass. They liked to sneak a quick shot before the club opened up. The metal fan rattled trying to beat back the sun. The weatherman said they were in store for a scorcher. It was supposed to hit a hundred and one.

Joan sat there stiff with her gold cigarette lighter. Her long legs were crossed, her nails immaculate. She wore a tight pencil skirt and a white low-cut Danskin. Though her wig was pinned up off the back of her neck, her scalp heated up like a skillet. She kept studying the room like she smelled something bad and kept wiping her lap with a napkin. She would only visit her sister in the day while the club was all closed. She thought the women at Dee's were beneath her and cheap. Joan would never be caught dead in Dee's Parlor at night.

Pearl pulled open a drawer and peered deep inside. She brought out a giant stack of old mail. One by one she held each piece to the sun.

"What in God's name are you looking for, Pearl?" Joan asked.

"Tony's not slick. Something's here, I can feel it. He shipped Miss Dee off to some home who knows where and I swear I will look till I find it. 'Member what Mama used to say to us all the time? If you keep looking, nine times out of ten, you bound to stumble on something." Pearl's glasses slipped farther down her nose.

Joan looked at her sister like she was a fool. "Nine times out of ten you'll find something you don't want. Admit it, you like snooping in other folks' junk. You're like an old dog gumming away at some shoes."

Joan sipped her drink. She twirled her gold lighter. She noticed the chipped plates and wobbly-looking chairs. "How can you work here? This place is a dump."

"'Cause, if I stay, I may find something out about Miss Dee and I'ma keep looking until it's all said and done."

Joan shook her head in disgust and popped open her compact. She urgently started plucking hairs from her chin. "Growing old ain't no joke. Tony sure dogged Miss Dee bad."

"Acting all slick just to get in that will," Pearl

said. "'Member what Sally Jenkins did to poor ol' Mr. Wade?"

"Dumb man shouldn't have trusted her with all his life savings! That bitch woulda pinched a penny from a dirty hog's ass."

"That's the same thing Tony did to Miss Dee. The last time I saw her I asked her point-blank, I said, 'Excuse me for prying and I mean no disrespect, but that man ain't worth spit and I know folks, Miss Dee. Been working here too long to let it go down like this. Every time I see that fool he got his hand out and you keep greasin' it like some damn Vaseline.' You know what she told me?"

"What?"

"Told me Tony was nice." Pearl sneered.

"Nice! Did you tell her that man's half iguana?" Joan opened her compact again and dabbed on more lipstick. "The man's skin's so thick I bet he can't even bleed."

Pearl adjusted the pull of her giant bra strap; it snapped against the skin on her shoulder. "I remember telling Miss Dee, you know what I told her?"

"What?"

"I said, 'Miss Dee, he's stealing.'"

"You told Miss Dee that?"

"Sure did," Pearl said. "But she didn't do shit." Pearl downed her shot and wiped off her lip. "She told me she knows. 'Been knowing,' she said. Said the little bit he takes she don't miss."

"Little bit!" Joan screamed. "Shit, the man has it all!"

"She told me Tony was the only one that comes by to see her. Said he perked up her day. Girl, you should have seen her smile. It gave me a window to the girl she once was."

"Tony drove all her good friends away. Always hanging at her door like some old hungry vulture. No one wanted to see Miss Dee with his big ass around."

"The ones bold enough to come, he wouldn't let get upstairs. He just takes their plates of food and don't even say thanks, lets the screen door smack back in their faces." Pearl studied Joan's face. She watched her and waited.

"Trudy tried to see her once," Pearl continued softly. "Told me Tony got out of line."

"And you believed her. Girl, you know how she lies. She must have led Tony on."

"Led him on! Tony don't need any leading."

"But you've seen her, Pearl. Look at her power around men. They can't keep their eyes off her. I've seen grown men turn right into putty. At ten years old, when some of my men friends came over, I swear, I just turned my back for two minutes and Trudy was in the man's lap."

"That's not power! Them grown men were

bothering her, Joan! She told me about your men friends," Pearl said knowingly.

Joan glared at her sister but let the comment drop. And the big thing they weren't saying finally came up, like the spins after a night getting smashed.

"You shouldn't have thrown her out," Pearl scolded her sister. "Trudy's too damn young to be out on the street."

"Bullshit, you and me were out at sixteen." Joan flicked the tall flame from her shiny gold lighter. "Trudy's twenty. That ain't hardly too young."

"Being out was a helluvalot different back then," Pearl said.

"Shoot, when you kicked Johnny out I didn't say boo! I let you handle your business. That was your son."

"I wish you'da said something." Pearl sadly stuck her hand in a big bowl of chips. "He's been locked up in Chino ever since." Pearl hated this subject. She'd tried to bring it up before but Joan cussed her and hung up the phone.

"Why are you tripping? Trudy's only been gone a few months."

"It's been well over a year and I'm worried about that girl. She's gravitating to the wrong kind." Pearl angrily munched on her chips.

"Look, she's grown. My job is finished. Why

are you jumping in stuff when you don't have the facts?"

"What facts?" Pearl asked. "What the hell did she do?"

Truth was, Joan knew exactly why she'd made Trudy leave. Trudy was in her way. She blocked what Joan really wanted. See, Hall told her he'd leave his wife once Trudy was gone. But Joan couldn't tell Pearl any of that, so she decided to fabricate a story.

"She was stealing!" Joan said. "I caught her red-handed myself. The police were bound to be knocking on my door."

Trudy was stealing, but Joan didn't know that. Pearl quietly poured them both drinks from the pitcher of margaritas and shook some more chips in a bowl.

Joan opened her compact and patted her heavily made-up face. "Greedy folks always get caught left and right. Some folks can't work next to all that stuff. Thieving fever sets in. If I've seen it once, I've seen it a hundred times. Oh, they get away at first. Steal a few things; let their friends shove a pair of pants in the bag. But they always got caught. Greed caught their ass in the end. I remember this guy. Oh, man, was he crazy. He kept filling bag after bag after bag. Talking all the time about how easy it was. But that fool couldn't stop. It was never enough. That Oriental rug was where he crossed the damn line. You can't steal a thousand-dollar rug and not expect red flags to go up. They took that fool boy out in handcuffs." Joan sat perched on her stool like a queen and took a neat sip from her glass.

"I remember that guy. He took you to nice west side restaurants."

"Had the nerve to ask me for three hundred dollars. Fool wanted me to come bail his ass out," Joan said dryly. "Only thing he got was a piece of my mind."

"That was that rich fella lived over there in Hancock Park, right?"

"Rich, hell. He wasn't doing nothing but fronting. Had the tiniest house on the whole fucking block. Told me he couldn't bear to tell his mama he stole. Skinny, stuck-up boy with big Coke-bottle glasses. Bragging all the time 'bout his argyle socks, like anybody gave a hot damn!"

"You were stealing, too. You used to get lots of stuff."

"The hell I was!" Joan snapped back. She crushed her butt in the ashtray.

"Thievin' fever has always run in this family." Pearl slowly stood up and emptied the ashtray. "No use tryin' to deny it with me."

It was never really talked about, but all of them did it. Switching tags, grabbing an extra pair of shoes. All of them came home with bags. "Oh, I got this or I got that," someone would say.

No one asked where or ever asked how. All they saw growing up was price tags getting ripped off with teeth late at night or burned loose with cigarette lighters in cars so they could wear the clothes right away. Their mother claimed it was because they were all born on that new stolen bed. She got the bed hot out the back of a Beakins moving van. Some roughnecks had robbed the big furniture store and their mama, the neighborhood bookie at the time, heard about it and asked for first dibs.

"Uh-uh. Don't point your finger at me. I know what you're thinking, and you're out of your mind. Trudy didn't get none of that stealing from me. You and Sonny was doing it. That was you all. Don't put me in the middle of that mess." Joan sat up and recrossed her shapely legs tight.

"Me and Sonny was doing it! Well, ain't this a bitch. Girl, that hot comb musta burnt what was left of your mind."

Joan snapped her compact and pursed her tight lips. "That was you all. That wasn't me, I remember. That was Sonny and y'all."

"Well, I remember when Mama had to drive across town." Pearl picked up a chip and munched it right in Joan's face. "Picked yo' thievin' ass up from the West L.A. station."

"That wasn't me, that was Sonny and them."

"That was Sonny and *you*! I remember that

night. You and Sonny thought y'all was slick in that Italian man's store. I know you remember that little turquoise suit, don't you? I bet that shit's still in your closet."

Joan stared at her drink and slowly stirred her red straw. "That was only one time. I wasn't bad like you guys."

"Shoot, I remember that and some other times too. Like me and you in that new jewelry store off Third. Slid that gold saffron ring right inside your big jaw. Mashed it inside that wad of gum you was always chewing on back then." Pearl slumped her large body back against her chair. "Wore that ring and that gold kitty necklace for years. Only stopped 'cause your neck got fat when you got pregnant."

Joan couldn't argue but wasn't about to be outdone.

"Oh, and what about you? Think you're so high and mighty. Miss Dee had some pretty nice fur coats at her house. What the hell happened to them?"

"Miss Dee was my friend. Me and her was tight. Besides"—Pearl looked down and gave a pitiful smile—"I'm sure she'da liked me to have 'em."

"Liked you to have 'em. Don't that beat all! You just up and helped yourself! That's what yo' thievin' ass did." Joan grabbed the bottle and poured herself a long shot. "Probably got 'em shoved inside that armoire of Mother's."

"Why you gotta bring up that armoire again?

You know Mama gave the armoire to me. You got the china cabinet. Got the butcher block too. Why you gotta bring up the armoire?"

"'Cause you took it! You know Mama said it was mine!"

Pearl didn't like being backed against the wall. "Well, at least I know where to draw the damn line. I don't steal other folks' husbands."

"I didn't take him!"

"Yes, you did!"

"The fuck I didn't!" Joan swore.

Pearl raised both her eyebrows and stared Joan down hard. "Then how do you explain Mr. Hall?"

"I didn't take him! I had him first." Joan stuck out her jaw and took a bite into her chip. "As far as I'm concerned the woman gave him to me. Holding out on sex is like taking a man's plate. Even a dog's got to go and eat somewhere." Joan downed the rest of her drink and threw Pearl a naughty smile.

"Amen," Pearl said, taking a handful of chips too. She was glad to reach some kind of truce.

Pearl got up and opened a tall wooden cabinet. She was rummaging around, peering deeply inside when Trudy walked into the room. Joan saw her come in and quickly stood up. Pearl shut the cabinet and frowned at her sister, holding her arm for her to stay. She wished Joan and Trudy could get along better. She didn't like her young niece living in an apartment alone. Especially in the beat cockroach street where she stayed. There were too many hoodlums hanging around. She worried more about Trudy each day.

"Hey, Trudy," Pearl said, trying hard to break the ice. "Come and give your ol' auntie a kiss."

Trudy'd been listening inside the club the whole time. She liked to eavesdrop on her mother when she talked. She was desperately searching for some kind of clue as to why her mother hated her so.

Trudy eyed Pearl and glanced quickly to her mother. She thought about what Vernita had told her in the car. She would try. She would at least try to talk to her mother. Maybe by now she'd calmed down.

"Hello, Mother. I got you that fragrance you like." Trudy opened her purse and pulled out a blue bottle.

"My Sin! Oh, girl, yo' mama loves that scent." Pearl smiled hopefully at Joan.

But Joan stood still. She didn't even flinch. So Pearl rushed up and grabbed the whole bottle. "Ooh, look at it, Joan, even the bottle looks sweet." Pearl tried to put the blue bottle inside Joan's hand. But Joan moved away and wouldn't take it.

"Come on, Joan. Smell it, it's nice." Pearl tried again to hand it to Joan, but Joan snatched her hand away so fast, the bottle crashed to the floor.

The whole room filled with its thick floral scent. Trudy stared down at her shoes.

"Joan! Oh my goodness, what's wrong with you, huh?" Pearl frowned at her sister. "This stuff ain't cheap." Pearl tried to save what was left in the bottle.

"That's okay," Trudy said meekly. Her lids began to well, so she bit on her tongue and squeezed the thin handles of her lime leather purse.

Joan picked up her clutch and tucked it under her arm. Her eyes rested at Trudy's large chest. Joan shook her head like Trudy's breasts were disgusting. Joan's own breasts were lifted to unimaginable heights, supported by a phenomenally large padded bra.

"Why do you like wearing all those godawful braids? You look like Kunta Kente." Joan jerked her keys out of her purse. A giant Mercedes emblem hung from the chain. It was scuffed on one side, like her car.

"Come on, Joan, they look nice. All the girls got 'em now." Pearl tried her best to get her sister to stay. "You don't have to go, rest your feet a hot minute. Happy hour's about to start. I'll fix us a nice little snack." Pearl stopped rummaging in a drawer and pulled on her apron.

When Joan drank, she got angry and lost her poised speech. "Stay for what? Some shriveled-up pigs feet and ribs? Shit, ain't nothing at this bar but some common, loud-mouthed bitches and hustlers looking for marks. All of them have butcher knives for hearts."

Joan checked the gold watch on the inside of her wrist. She took a deep breath and regained her composure. "No, I have to go," Joan calmly told them. "I've got to take my three o'clock bath." She glanced at Trudy, then quickly away. "I like to keep mine nice and fresh."

When the floor creaked, Pearl slammed the drawer closed with her hip. Tony strolled into the room. He was holding a beer and an Oreo box. He looked at Trudy, then Pearl and a long time at Joan, like he'd finally found his true target.

"It smells like a got damn whorehouse in here!" Tony twisted the black cookie and licked off the white frosting. "Well, I'll say, Miss Thang came to pay me a visit." Tony let his gaze roam over Joan's pulled-tight blouse. "Your ass always been nice and fresh to me."

Joan stared at Tony like he was a stray dog. To her he was nothing but cheap, lowlife scum. Speaking to him was hardly worth the effort.

"What? You can't speak? You too high-toned to talk? Well, I remember a time when you wasn't."

In a drunken moment long ago, Joan had gone home with Tony. It was a night she steadfastly denied in her head.

Tony's eyes never left Joan's tall, shapely

frame. "Your baby girl's packing 'em in here each night." Tony licked the rest of the sweet white from the cookie. "I told 'em she learned from the best."

Joan sneered at Tony's hideous face. She glided across the room like a high-fashion model. But before she reached the door she stopped and turned around. "How's Flo?" Joan boldly asked Tony. She grinned as the pain began to weigh in Tony's face.

"Oh, that's right." Joan smiled more broadly. "I'm sorry, I forgot. Pearl, what's his name? You know, the postal worker, the well-built, super-fine, young-looking one? The one who knocks the hot breath from your lungs."

Pearl smiled at Joan. She knew exactly what Joan was doing. "Oh, yeah, that's right, pretty boy, gorgeous fellow. Make a woman want to pee when she see him." Pearl glanced at the ceiling as if she were thinking. "Let me see what's his name? I think it starts with a C."

"Oh, that's right." Joan smiled brightly. "How could I forget—Charles. The Lord didn't make many like him. Flo's with Charles. Yeah, that's right. They make such a nice couple. She's a little older, but hell, I tip my hat to that girl. She knows how to keep a man happy." Joan watched the small muscles in Tony's face tighten. Her own face changed into a savage, cruel grin. She threw her scarf around her neck and left.

Tony looked at Trudy and quickly at Pearl before taking his cookie box upstairs.

"What does Tony know about Mama?" Trudy asked.

"Nothing. Tony's just talking." Pearl started wiping the tabletop clean.

"Mama used to steal?" Trudy asked her point-blank.

But Pearl was uncomfortable talking about Trudy's mother. "We was all young fools back then, baby."

Trudy looked at the bar's colorful bottles of liquor. "I remember a time I saw Mama take something."

Pearl turned around and walked toward the small closet. She didn't like talking to her niece about that mess. Some things were best left unsaid.

"It was right when Mama first started seeing Mr. Hall."

"Hall ain't nothing but a fuckin' loan shark. Gave everyone credit." Pearl grabbed a broom and started sweeping the floor. "Then he sucks out the blood on those month-to-month notes. Look what he done to your mother."

"I remember the collectors kept calling all the time."

"Yo' mama went through hell way back then, baby. Lockheed shut down and your daddy lost his aerospace factory job. When he died, the state took the house."

"We moved to that tiny liquor store apartment upstairs. Mr. Hall would visit. He'd give Mama credit. All day and night our phone would just ring. She told me don't answer it, used to cover it with pillows, but one time Mama just couldn't stand it no more. She put on her black pumps, grabbed my hand and her purse and we went to go see Mr. Hall." Trudy sat down and picked up a chip.

"She was driving so fast, I really got scared. Cussing at the traffic and slamming the brakes. When her nylons got ripped she stopped off at Rite-Aid and helped herself to a new pair of queen-size pantyhose. She shoved the thin package inside my pink sweater. I was young and didn't know why she put them in there. So when we got to the door, I pulled the stockings back out and said, 'Mommy, we still have to buy these.'"

"She told me 'bout that." Pearl laughed as she swept a bent broom across the floor. "Your mama was fit to be tied."

"I'll never forget that hard look on her face. When we got to the lot, Mama pulled off one shoe. She whipped me right there, right between the parked cars. I had heel marks on my legs for weeks."

Pearl put the broom down. She'd hadn't heard that part.

"Your mama was under a lot of stress, baby." Pearl swept without offering anything further.

"I waited in the receptionist area and could hear them arguing inside. They stayed in his office for hours. When she came out, her lipstick was smeared and her dress was all twisted but her fist clutched a handful of bills."

"Your mama been slick like that from day one," Pearl said.

Trudy picked up a chip and snapped it in half. Trudy remembered when she'd started taking things from Mr. Hall's office. When she took things she felt like she was paying him back for taking the good part of her mother. She'd take quarters and all of his really nice pens, anything she found in the drawer. One day she even took Mr. Hall's family picture. She took it right out from its shiny gold frame. She folded it up in her white lacy sock and buried it in the yard when she got home.

"As soon as we moved here, everything changed. Mama got mean. She hated everything I did."

"Mr. Hall moved y'all but kept his other whole family," Pearl said. "I think that just about killed your poor mother. That and seeing you in his lap."

Trudy bit her lip. She shifted her purse on her arm. "I was fourteen," Trudy said, trying to hide a weak smile. "Hall wanted to know how much I weighed." Trudy remembered that day well. She'd felt a delirious sick pleasure. She'd had both her thick arms around Mr. Hall's neck.

She could tell he was scared. She could feel his legs twitch. But for a split second she'd finally beaten her mother at something. She knew it was mean and it was only one time, but for a moment, while she sat, watching her mother's pained face, it was the most triumphant time of her life.

"That just about blew your poor mother's mind. She sat right in here and drank back-to-back shots of bourbon. And you know what she thinks about Dee's."

"I think Mama thinks he touched me, but the lap thing was it. He came every Sunday, right after church, and from then on I stayed in my room. He took Mama and me to church when his wife was on trips. Those church ladies looked like they might gash out our eyes. They never spoke once. Didn't invite us to nothing. If they saw Mama first they would always cross the street."

"Sometimes church can be a good place for evil to hide," Pearl told her. "Y'all wasn't missing too much."

"Mama tried to act like she was better than those ladies. She tried to dress expensive, pretended to be rich. She slaved over her clothes to keep them all looking perfect."

"Looks like you got that in common," Pearl said, smiling.

Trudy smoothed out her tight lavender skirt.

"Your mother was something else back when

we was both young. Had the finest legs walkin'. Brothas used to line up. I was the short one. Had my few stragglers." Pearl smiled and fanned herself with a menu. "But your mama was tall. She could have been a star. Had a smile that could melt hard candy right in the jar."

"Well, what happened? How'd she get so mean?" Trudy bit into a chip. A few crumbs dropped to her lap.

"She ain't mean. Yo' mama just picked the wrong man. Wanting the wrong thing can ruin yo' life." Pearl stared at the club's water-stained ceiling. "If you walk with your head stuck in a cloud all the time, eventually you bound to trip and fall. Your mother stumbled on Mr. Hall."

Trudy thought her mother was the biggest fool on earth. "Why doesn't she leave him? What does she see? Everyone knows that he's married!"

"Her heart don't know yet," Pearl said, lowering her eyes. "Love is like gin. It's so clear, you can't see it. But Lord, you can sho' feel its heavy, hot taste. If you forget that bottle, or leave off the top, eventually it evaporates away. Yo' mama spilt her bottle a long time ago. I never liked Hall, used to call him Alaska. I never met a soul that damn cold. Old Hall stripped all the warm fire from yo' mama. Each time she sees him he sucks out more blood."

"All I know is she picked Mr. Hall over me."

"She didn't pick you or Hall, she was picking

herself. Your mama was one to want things. Always loved her possessions. Even when we was young she had to have the best. Hall lets her have whatever she wants but won't give her what really matters."

"Well, I'm taking my shit. I'm not waiting for no man. Come slap me if I ever end up that dumb." Trudy went to the dressing room and slammed the small door. She swore she'd never be anything like her mother. Her mother was weak. People laughed behind her back. She was a home-wreckin' sneak taking three o'clock baths. Trudy would never mess around with another woman's man. Trudy had standards. That's why she had a plan. But even the greatest of plans had to make some exceptions. Sometimes you didn't cross it but got close to the line. Like taking something once but then putting it back. Borrowing it like you might do a library book. Not stealing, just holding it for a hot minute. Trudy's hot minute was Charles.

# 8

## Charles and Tony

Big Percy, a former boxer, manned the gambling door at Dee's. He was refrigerator-wide, with one crazy, wandering eye and a birthmark across his top lip. Once you entered Dee's doors, the first thing you saw was Percy. If you wanted to gamble, he led you behind black velvet drapes, hiding a large heavy gate, which led to a narrow flight of stairs. Percy would slowly click the latch on the metal-caged door. The door made an awful grating sound when it opened. He'd pat you down fast. Pat, pat, pat. Shoulders, waist, thighs, then he'd yell back to the boys inside, "Coming in!" You had to be real careful in a gambling house. You didn't want any cops or rowdy fools wearing guns.

Charles ran upstairs and took a spot at the table. It wasn't really a table but a large piece of plywood, covered in olive-green felt. The room was smoke-filled and dense with loud-talking men. A fan blew the dead, boozy air in his face. Charles was so anxious to win, his whole back was broken out in sweat. He tossed down two hundred and took a gulp from someone's bottle. In six minutes, Charles lost over four hundred dollars. When he crept back downstairs and went inside the club, he hoped Tony would give him a scotch on the house.

Tony spotted Charles sitting at a table alone. In the fifteen short minutes Charles had been at Dee's Parlor, he'd already lost all his money.

"I gotta cool game upstairs, man, if you want to sit in. Some high-rollers just came through the gate."

But Charles didn't have anything to gamble with now. The quarters he had on him danced a sad, empty tune with the few loose nickels and dimes.

"No, man, I'm cool." Charles looked away from Tony. "But I need to talk to you a minute."

"What's the matter, bro, y'all have a midnight spat?" He slapped Charles's back and laughed real loud, his throat wheezing like he had asthma. Tony eyed him sidewise as Charles was shifting in the seat. Tony could see Charles had something on his mind.

"Hey, Earl! Bring me one of them bottles for my boy here, and don't let Stan go behind the bar." Tony put his arm around Charles. They were sitting at a small table close to the stage. A trio was playing John Coltrane.

"Flo wearing you down, man? That's all right, son. Here. Have some of this." He took a deep swig, wiped his mouth with his sleeve and poured the dark liquid inside Charles's glass.

"Now see, that's why I don't live with no damn woman now. Who wants to see the same raggedy ass every morning? I like having me a stable myself. I got this one chick got a husband work thirty years for Pac Bell, says he's boring as hell. She be out there every morning with a worn housedress on, smiling while handing him his lunch bag. I creep over there 'bout an hour after her ol' man leaves. She be all dolled up to see my butt too. Shoot, I don't have to take her to lunch, dinner or nothing. Bring my own flask and take it back home. Don't nobody bother me for shit."

Charles downed the rest of his drink and held the empty glass in his hand. His mind was consumed with his looming gambling debt. He avoided looking in Tony's eyes.

Tony poured them both another stiff round.

"Flo's been tripping out lately," Charles said, steering the subject. He didn't want to bring up the subject of money. Charles had gotten himself in a mess. Charles loved cash like young girls love clothes. Though he borrowed, he never paid anyone back. It's not like he couldn't. He definitely made enough. His postal job paid him a nice hefty check. And his benefits were the best in the state. But Charles always wanted something. He shopped all the time. He liked stereo equipment and forty-inch screens. He liked appliance shops and outdoor furniture sets. He didn't buy any of these items. Charles wasn't a hoarder. He just admired all these things when he saw them in stores.

See, Charles wanted a house. He was saving his money. He only window-shopped, dreaming of what to put inside. He saved all his money with a fiendish conviction. He cringed if Flo asked him to give up a dime. To him, giving money was like peeling off his skin. Their apartment was a sparse nest of wobbly chairs and lamps you had to bang with your hand to turn on.

But everything changed when he started betting at Dee's. Charles had never won anything before in his life. He wasn't a gambler. Gamblers were weak. They were slick toothpick types with gold teeth. To this day, he couldn't say why he drifted to the room upstairs. Maybe it was the men whooping wild or the clanking of bottles and the sound of people having big fun. Charles couldn't remember the last time he'd had a good time. The monotony of his postal job stripped the fun from his life, like the sun did his faded gray pants. The next thing he knew, someone handed him the dice. People smiled as he rattled the dice in his hand. He spun them hard, letting them dance across the smooth green. He didn't do it once, he did it time and again, and each time the crowd roared and cheered in his ear. He was winning. Charles could barely believe his eyes. In no time he had a huge stack of chips. There was nothing in life close to how good he felt then. He came day after day trying to feel that good again, but in no time he owed Tony thousands. But Tony didn't sweat him. He even let him play on credit. That's why he sat and endured Tony's bad breath. That's why he let Tony drape his arm around his shoulders. Maybe Tony would forget. Maybe he wouldn't have to pay him. It killed him to think of giving his savings away. Charles sloshed his drink across his straight, perfect teeth. Tony's breath stunk but Charles just sat there and took it. Making Tony his friend might erase his bad debt.

"Damn," Charles said, following Tony down to the bar. "Lady Luck ain't with me today."

"Nigga, please, you don't have to tell me. Lady Luck is just like any other kind of woman. Love 'em; leave 'em, none of 'em any good. I swore off them hags a long time ago. That's why I steal all of my pussy now. I don't have to hear no nagging or nothing. Nobody asking me to take the trash out or mow the damn lawn." Tony tapped out a Winston and jammed it in the side of his mouth. He leaned back in his chair and his shirt rode up his gut, which brimmed massively over his pants. "The onliest thing I hear when I walk

118

through that door is the smack of my screen, the gush of me pouring myself a shot and the click when I hit the remote.

"Listen," Tony said, edging his chair closer to Charles's shoulder, "let me peep you some game on how to get Flo right." Tony leaned in toward Charles. Got right in his throat. The blue light in the room gave Tony's face a monstrous glow, and his silhouette bounced across the back wall of the stage.

"What you need, what you want, is a side woman, son. A side woman's known to cure all problems at home." Tony gulped down his drink and flicked his long ash. His Winston was down near the filter. When he exhaled the smoke, Tony started to choke. He wheezed and coughed hard for such a long time, Charles wondered if homeboy was dying. "Mark my words, son," Tony said, holding in his smoke. "Competition'll make any woman stop and take note. A side woman will drop Flo back down a few notches. Watch. You gotta know how to play the game, son." Tony's grin revealed a row of giant buckteeth, sporting plenty of juicy pink gums.

When Charles didn't say a thing, Tony changed the subject.

"So who you got for the fight coming up, man? Everybody in town say Liston'll have him down in five, but Jones ain't no city-boy neither. I hear them country fools box all the mules and mares down there. He's liable to do some real damage to Liston. Odds say he'll go down in eight."

"Man, I haven't been following it much," Charles replied, casting his eyes to the ground. He didn't want to talk about gambling. He was way down already. He swallowed the few drops that were left in his glass and dabbed his face with his napkin.

Charles avoided Tony's eyes. He tried to act upbeat.

Tony studied Charles for a very long time. "I can go ahead and place what you owe if you want," Tony said. He glanced over at Percy, who nodded his head.

Charles looked up. So Tony did remember the debt. Charles looked like someone standing in oncoming traffic.

"Don't worry, Youngblood, you'll get it to me," Tony said, smiling. He patted Charles's back and abruptly stood up. Tony talked to Big Percy, who nodded again, watching the club and guarding the gambling door with prison-guard eyes.

"Oh, it's cool," Charles, said, dabbing his brow. Shoot, if need be, he would have to take the money from savings. That's only if Tony sweated him, but if Charles played him right he might not. Charles couldn't see the heat in Big Percy's stare.

# WANT SOME

Suddenly the lights dimmed into one beaming ray. Maybe Tony was right. A side woman might be just what he needed again. Something to take off the pressure and stress. He watched Trudy glow under the single white halo, and like a platinum lighter she shined in Dee's haze. When she smiled she looked like she was smiling at him. Oh, he'd seen her before. Seen her a whole bunch of times. But tonight she looked different. She sparkled somehow. Tonight she looked something like hope.

# 9

## *Charles and Flo*

It was a month and two weeks since Charles had flung that bottle. And as Trudy planned her scam, Charles's gambling reached the brink. But Flo didn't know any of that. All she remembered was the loud, violent crash. In fact, the very next day, Flo went straight to the bank and drained every cent they had. She knew what she wanted. Had already been to the dealer. She wanted a cool, ice-blue, chrome-rimmed Camaro. The dealer told her he'd hold it. He said he'd Teflon the seats, tint all the windows and throw in Lo-Jack in case it got stolen. Flo knew they were supposed to use that money to move, but when that glass bottle crashed all over her head, Flo went straight to the bank and said, "Fuck it."

"Fool better know not to mess over me," Flo

said, seething. She flashed everyone in the bank line a cold, evil eye. She didn't want to chitchat or have to fake smile. All Flo wanted to get was that money.

See, that Jack Daniels bottle was Flo's final straw. Glass in her hair and all through her clothes. No, Flo's mind was made up. She didn't rip up his shirts or burn the hems of his pants. She didn't put sand in his shoes or white salt in his tank. No, this time Flo headed straight to the bank to take every cent they had out.

"Get his money," her grandmother said about Charles. "You want to stab a man smack-dab in his heart, go mess around with his cash."

See, it wasn't really the bottle that led to Flo's wrath. The bottle only ignited a simmering rage. An anger so bitter it was hard to keep down, and it burned like a Malibu fire.

Flo took Venice to Midtown where it hits San Vicente. It was hot, but luckily she made all the lights and in no time her tires were at Wilshire. She turned left and hooked another quick right, pulling into the Bank of America's opulent lot. The lot was packed. It was brimming with new, gleaming cars. Porsches, Bentleys, Mercedes-Benz, Range Rovers and Town Cars with drivers. Flo got out, giving the parking attendant her keys and taking the elevator up to the lobby. When she got inside the door, Flo took a deep breath. The air conditioner's full blast cooled down her skin. Flo walked in holding her purse snug against her arm. It was a large bank with huge murals and expansive marble floors. The tellers sat behind gold inlaid counters.

Flo stood there until the bell tone signaled her turn. Flo was digging in her purse for the tiny bank book when she looked up to the teller's glass window.

"May I help you?" Trudy smiled at Flo.

Flo just about dropped her purse.

"Yes . . . yes," she stammered. "I need to make a withdrawal. I'd like to close out this account." Flo pushed the yellow bank slip under the glass and pretended to study her own shoes.

Keeping her head down, Flo fiddled with the bank teller's pen. She felt uncomfortable looking Trudy in the face. She knew she worked at the club, and there was a good chance she knew Charles. She didn't want her to ask any questions.

"Is this a joint account?" Trudy asked.

"No," Flo told her flatly.

But on the computer screen, Trudy saw Charles's name. "Well, you'll both need to come in to close this completely."

"Why?" Flo asked point-blank. "My name's on it too. I don't see why there's a problem."

Flo stared at Trudy. She felt nervous and worried. *This bitch is trying to fuck with me, I know it.*

"I'm sorry," Trudy said, typing something on the screen.

"This is a trip—you take my money when I come in alone but you need both of us when it comes to getting it back out." Flo glanced at the people waiting behind her in line. She felt anxious. Something about this felt wrong. Maybe Trudy knew something; maybe she didn't want her to have the cash. Trudy picked up a receiver and started to dial. Maybe she was calling Charles right now on that phone.

Trudy hung up the line and smiled at Flo. "You can withdraw, but you need to leave some of it in so the account is not totally closed."

"Well, how much do you need me to leave?" Flo asked.

"The minimum is five dollars," Trudy said coolly.

Flo was the one who smiled this time. "I think five dollars is fine."

Flo pushed another yellow withdrawal slip through the opening with the new amount as $7,995.

Trudy stared at the computer screen again. She put a small slip inside a miniature printer. She wrote something down on a ledger.

"How would you like it?" she suddenly asked.

Whoa, Flo breathed out. She was getting the money! Flo smiled again while nervously watching the door. If Charles came in she surely would be busted. She wanted to hurry up and go.

Flo unzipped the side pocket of her purse to get it ready. "Big bills," Flo quickly said and looked down. Flo kept her lids down. She watched Trudy's hands. Trudy opened a drawer, pulling a bundle of hundreds. She skillfully counted out each thousand-dollar stack. When she reached seven, she moved that whole stack aside. Then she counted out nine hundreds and moved that stack too. Then she opened the drawer again and got out four twenties, one ten and one single five. She put the whole stack in the bank teller slot, and Flo took it before Trudy let go of it good.

"Is there anything else I can help you with today?" Trudy asked, smiling.

Flo smiled too, but she didn't mean it. It was the kind of smile you gave someone you didn't like. "Yeah" Flo wanted to say, "stay the hell away from my man."

"No, thank you," Flo told her, zipping her purse closed. "I think this will be fine."

Flo turned and quickly walked toward the bank door. She looked back and saw Trudy's tongue race across her glossed lips. A white, tan-suit man now stood in her line. Trudy grinned at the man, flinging her braids across her chest. Flo smacked the elevator button and went down.

Flo couldn't believe how easy getting the new car was. In no time at all she was in the front seat. The smile on her face was real this time as she watched the salesman wipe off the fender and side mirrors.

As soon as her tires left the lot, Flo felt a hell

of a lot better. When she got to the freeway she felt like a star. The new car made her feel she had finally arrived. Like she'd risen above Charles's trifling behind. She wasn't somebody you tossed liquor bottles at either. She had worth. She deserved something clean and expensive. The car told the world she was someone with value. That she was the one in the driver's seat now. That Flo was the only one calling the shots, even if she stopped twice to pull over and cry.

Because even as she drove the new car toward the beach, as its dazzling paint battled with the burning hot sun, as its gleaming chrome rims beat against the black pavement, Flo felt a sadness creeping in through the vents. A sadness she'd been masking from last year to now. It smothered her heart, drained the blood from her face, like a fog hovering over a grave.

See, from last year to now, everything went down. This time last year, everything changed. That's when a boiling flame engulfed her. It scorched her whole heart. That's when Charles went and fucked him that white girl.


Last year, Flo showed up unexpectedly at Charles's job. He always took his lunch break at the McDonald's on Western. Flo borrowed a friend's car to surprise him there. When she walked in the restaurant, she didn't see Charles at first. Then her eyes found a table way toward the back. There was Charles, but he wasn't sitting alone. Both his arms were wrapped around this big, garish blonde and he was grinning like some Uncle Tom slave. Flo never in her life felt a raw hurt like that. When Flo walked over, the blond girl leaped up and ran. Charles sat there and smiled, didn't try to deny it. He just looked at her with a sick little smirk on his face, saying, "Baby, I wish you'd a called first."

Lord have mercy, Flo never knew she could hurt bad like that. A white girl. Charles went and got him a Barbie! A fucking white skank ho and Charles. Well, Charles might as well have just stabbed her right there. 'Cause it sure killed something way deep down in Flo. Something that gnawed at her, tore at the core of her heart. Something she never got back.

In fact, after that day, they were never the same. She remembered how she felt before she walked through that door. She was beaming with pride. Had a sweet secret present. Flo had come to his job to tell Charles she was pregnant. It was supposed to be a surprise. But when Flo saw that white chick wrapped up in his arms, saw him stroking her long hair that hung limp like a skunk, Flo never said nothing. She never told Charles at all. She walked out the door and drove straight to the clinic. She paid four hundred dollars and lay on a white sheet. She watched the doctor's pink smock as she counted back from ten, and the next thing she knew, the whole world went black.

No matter how hard she tried, things were never right with her and Charles. Day after day she hated him more. And sometimes she'd lie up in bed late at night and think about slicing his throat. She became meaner inside, her head filled with cruel thoughts, and sometimes she'd do those things too. Last month she stole her co-worker's purse. It was something Flo never would have dreamed of before. But there the purse was in her drawer.

Heather kept her purse locked up in her desk with the small key dangling from her neck. Flo noticed one day that the drawer was slightly ajar. She looked around fast to see who was around and then scooped up the purse, slipped it inside her fat *L.A. Times*, sliding it back under her desk. At the end of the day, Flo watched Heather cry. Her blond hair stuck together in thick gooey chunks. She kept saying over and over, "It's gone, oh, my God!" Sobbing, with her head on her desk.

The company assumed the cleaning crew got it or the Xerox man snatched it. No one ever suspected her. When Flo got home she examined the purse's contents. She smiled to herself as she smelled the fine leather; she played with the keys and touched the tortoiseshell comb, running her fingers across its neat teeth. She

twisted open the pale Clinique lipsticks inside;
they were all the same dull shades of mauve.
Sometimes when Flo had the whole house to
herself, she'd take the purse out, touch the
items inside and then slam the purse back in her
closet.

Flo gripped the new steering wheel in her
hand. There weren't two ways about it. She had
to get this car. She deserved it for enduring all
that awful hard pain. Besides, if she didn't do
something about this bursting feeling she had,
someone was bound to get hurt.

# 10

## Tony and Flo

"My, my, my, Miss Flo. I always said you was a fine woman and can do some serious damage when you put your mind to it. Goodness!" Tony said, watching her pull in. "Car looks good on you, gal!" Tony pushed his gold sunglasses farther down on his nose.

Tony was sitting on the step waiting for her on her porch. He stood and tipped his brim hat as she parked.

*Damn.* Flo thought, slamming the car door shut. *What's this damn dog doing here?*

Flo passed by Tony and rolled her eyes.

"Whaz hap'nin, baby? Charles home yet? I knocked." Tony didn't step aside, and Flo's full body had to brush across his gut to get by.

"Not yet," she shot back, shifting a bag to her

hip. She could smell the booze eating through his skin.

"Oh, well," Tony said, smiling. "It's kinda late, ain't it? Post office must be backed up again."

"I guess Charles will get here when he gets here," Flo snapped again, not inviting Tony in.

"Hee, hee, that's if he comes straight home. You know some mens like to make a pit stop first, but I'm sure Charles ain't one of them. Oh, no, I wouldn't think he was." Tony gently sucked his thick bottom lip. "Shoot, if I had all this peach cobbler waiting on my porch, I'd punch out and race home every day."

Flo rolled her eyes at him again. She didn't like Tony. She didn't appreciate him coming around behind Charles's back, trying to flirt with her and act like he was Charles's friend. Flo had never told Charles about Tony and her. It was a long time ago and they weren't together long. Besides, Charles didn't need to know another thing he could throw in her face. So Flo skirted around Tony whenever he came by and told him to keep his mouth closed.

"Didn't I tell you not to come around here?" Flo reminded him.

"You worry too much, girl! Don't you know me yet? I'ma take that shit to the grave." Tony looked at her legs an extra-long time. "But you and me got history. That ain't gon' change. Just 'cause you don't want that nigga to know don't mean I'ma forget." Tony smiled looking deep in

Flo's dark, lovely eyes until she had to look down at the steps.

It was just like Tony to bring it up every time. Acting like he got extra privileges because they shared this secret. She didn't appreciate Tony coaxing Charles out to the club either. All that gambling mess and carrying on. Showing up in the middle of the night to collect.

One time Tony knocked on their door real late.

Flo was in her slip. It was what she liked to cook in on hot summer nights. The kind of night all your windows were slung open wide trying to catch a slim breeze. Where you opened the freezer to knock the heat from your skin. That night, Charles and Flo were sitting in the kitchen. He was watching her while listening to Sunday night slow jams. They were talking about their day. Having a glass of wine or two. Charles pouring her a glass. Her pouring his. The oven on and the radio crooning Al Green. The kitchen. Yeah. It was real cozy back then. The kitchen was always the heart of the house. She'd like to sit at her table with one foot on the stove. Bite into a peach; leave the juice on her cheek. She loved the sheer warmth of bread, happily soaking up butter. The dark, simple quietness of a drawer full of spoons. The hunger of forks trying to rest on their napkins. The glass melting wet in her hand.

It was one of those nights she and Charles

were messing around in the kitchen. Charles was at the table rolling a smoke, watching her mix the batter for a pie. He liked the way her breasts would shake ever so slightly as she kneaded the dough and how her nipples stood so firm in that satin. Charles got up and squeezed her soft, ample waist.

"Boy, you better quit. I'm trying to cook here," Flo said.

But when Charles saw her pressing that dough he couldn't help it. He stood up and circled her waist from behind, lavishly kissing her shoulders. He spread her across the flat kitchen table like Flo was hot margarine on toast. Next thing she knew the Crisco bottle spilled over and Flo felt the warm wet running way down her back, pooling inside her tight thighs. Charles grabbed the bottle and poured it over her stomach. He started kneading her breasts just as she had done the dough.

"You feel so good, baby," Charles moaned in her ear. Thrusting real nice and easy, the way he knew she liked it. "I could just swallow you whole."

Flo bent her knees way up to her chest and Charles went deeper inside. She rubbed Crisco on her hands and massaged his wide back, squeezing and kneading his skin. Charles was well-built and caramel, with a wide chest and strapping arms and a six-pack twisted as tight as a radiator cap. Flo had never in her life had a man that damn fine.

Charles pounded her harder and the table rattled so loud Flo was sure it would snap right in half. But she didn't care. She could feel the raw heat working up from her toes, lingering between the skin in her thick inner thighs and then raging on up toward her gut.

"Wait." The word barely escaped from her lips.

Charles tried to slow down but it was already too late. He had turned to pure steel; there was no stopping now. Once he got to this point there was no turning back. He was thrashing so strong the table skipped across the floor and smacked against the back wall.

Well, it was right then when they heard a weak knock at the door. Truth was, Tony had been out there for quite a good while. He crouched down and peeked into the window when he saw that the lights were off in all the rooms except the kitchen. He saw Flo's big legs dangling over the table and Charles standing between them. Tony lit a cigarette and took a gulp from his bottle. He tossed the bottle in the street and it crashed at the curb and then he banged real loud on the door.

Charles threw water on his face and answered the door. Tony saw Flo pulling her robe back together.

"Evening, everybody," Tony said, walking back toward the kitchen.

"Oh, y'all been making a pie!" Tony looked at the oil dripping down to the floor. "I sure hope I get a piece when you're through."

The way Tony said it made Flo suddenly look up. Like maybe he wasn't talking about no pie at all.

So when Flo saw Tony today she blocked Tony's path. He was always coming around, sniffing for crumbs. Like a cat you once threw a chicken leg to and now couldn't get off your porch.

"I wish you'd come down to the club sometime, baby. Trudy been packing 'em in left and right."

Flo ignored him. Wouldn't look in his face.

"Charles been catching all her shows. I don't know what he see. She don't do nothing for me, but I wouldn't let my man loose with that chick on the stage." Tony's eyes twinkled. He let that sink in. He eyed Flo's hips and studied her breasts. "But she don't hold a candle to you."

Flo didn't wait for him to say anything else. She went in and double-locked her front door.

Tony stared at the door for a real long time. He lit the burnt stub of his halfway-smoked Winston before stumbling back to his car. He stared at the moon and then at his shined shoes.

## WANT SOME

"As sure as I'm standing up out here tonight"—Tony blew the thick smoke back toward Flo's door—"I'ma have that damn heifer spread-eagled one day and calling me Daddy again."

# 11

## Trudy and Ray Ray

"Hey, fat back."
"Hey, pig meat."
"Gimme them big suck-me titties."

A small band of teenage boys lined the sidewalk. They followed her fast strut down the street.

"Trudy with the booty. Come gimme some, girl!"

Trudy tried to walk fast but they circled her body. She had to struggle to keep moving down the block.

"Look at 'em move."
"Do fries go with that shake, baby?"
"They look like a batcha grape Jell-O!"

The boys gathered tightly around her firm frame.

"Move!" Trudy said, but only a few of them budged.

"Oooh, see, she mad!"

"Look, watch 'em jiggle."

"Come on girl, we just want to suck 'em."

The boys busted up laughing and started nudging each other. Some of them had her nude videotape in their rooms.

"That movie's a'ight, but it ain't got shit on yo' ass in the flesh."

Trudy struggled her best to get past the boys. One sucked a Blow Pop. One held an apple. All of them had big, gaping grins. Two women watched from the safety across the street; one blew a giant pink bubble.

"Leave me alone!" Trudy screamed loudly. She struggled against them. Her nylons got snagged. A seam busted on her tight dress. But she flung out her purse like it was a weapon, swatting their heads until a few scattered back.

She'd almost broken free, but somebody tripped her and she landed facedown on the sidewalk. The boys made a knot around Trudy's body. Someone grabbed her ass. Someone else twisted her nipple. A slimy tongue entered her ear.

"Get off me!" she screamed. But the boys pinned her down.

Ray Ray stopped his Lincoln in the middle of the street. He sliced through the crowd of boys with his razor-blade eyes. One boy ran off. The others leaned back on their broomstick-thin legs.

"Hey, Ray Ray!"

"What up, cuz!"

"Nigga, when'd you get out, Gee!"

The boys looped around Ray Ray's muscle-bound body.

Ray Ray scowled at them all. He stared hard at one.

"Ain't you Smokey's little brother?" he asked him point-blank.

"Yeah," the short boy said proudly.

Ray Ray reached down and pulled Trudy up from the ground. He glared at each boy and lit a match to his Newport. He stuck the cigarette way back in his teeth and blew the smoke out real slow. He pulled a leather cloth out the back of his khakis and unwrapped a long steel blade. It shimmered in the cruel, blasting sun. He smacked the Blow Pop out of one of the boys' mouth. He knocked the apple from the other boy's fist.

"Pick it up!" Ray Ray said to another.

The worried boy put the apple in Ray Ray's hand.

Ray Ray started peeling the green apple with the silver blade. He never looked up. He just kept on cutting. He skinned the apple until it was totally clean. The curled skin dropped dead on the ground.

"See, this here's my homegirl." Ray Ray

pointed with his knife. His steely eyes cut each boy down. "I bet' not catch one y'all mutha-fuckas messin' with her again. Fool around and yo' mama's gon' be pickin' out caskets."

The neighborhood boys had fearful respect for Ray Ray. He was an O-G. He'd been to the pen. They all wanted to be Ray Ray's friend.

"It's cool, man," one said.

"We didn't mean nothin'."

The boys slowly drifted away.

"You better walk away!" Trudy shouted at their backs. "All y'all can do is try to hijack some pussy 'cause no women with any sense gonna touch ya!"

Ray Ray smiled at Trudy. Homegirl was a trip. Wasn't but five-three but talked mega shit if you crossed her. He loved sexy bitches like that.

Fact was, Trudy was the only one who'd writ-ten when he was in the pen. She didn't write often. And she didn't write much, but those let-ters were what kept Ray Ray together. Kept the monotony of bar after bar from closing in. Kept him focused on doing his time and getting out. No, she didn't write often but what she did write he read over and over again. Memorizing every word. Rolling over every curve of each letter with his finger. Mumbling each phrase with his lips.

"I appreciated your letters."

"No problem." Trudy smiled, pulling her braids from her face.

"A kind word from the outside can take a brother a long way." Ray Ray brushed a torn leaf off the back of her dress. She looked so good, his whole body ached just to watch her. He wanted to feel her smooth skin against his hot, scalded face. To taste her long braids between his teeth. Ray Ray looked at Trudy deeply, breathing out slow. "Your letters are what kept me alive."

Trudy didn't know a lot about his life in prison. Whenever he wrote, large parts were blacked out. But one thing came through remarkably clear. Ray Ray was smart. And he cared for her deeply. He would hide little messages inside the lines. His metaphors gave her a glimpse of the harsh world inside. They were a telephone line to his soul. That wasn't blacked out. The jailers never found those. CALIFORNIA STATE PRISON was stamped on each letter in red, but Trudy was proud when the postman handed her a letter from Ray Ray. She would spread across her bed and read them alone.

"Girl, I loved seeing my name on those envelopes you wrote." Ray Ray smiled at her again. "That alone was hope. They made me feel like I mattered. Most of them dudes don't never get shit. Nobody writes. Nobody calls. Them letters kept me from going off and hurtin' somebody. I saw brothas snap, every single day." Ray Ray broke a small branch from a tree. "Yesterday's gone and you can't swallow tomorrow." Ray Ray smiled broadly at Trudy again. "But I could reread your words. They always calmed me down. I'd stop thinking how I fucked up and ended up like this. How I did all this shit to my-self."

Trudy cupped his cheek. He wanted to kiss her hand, but he didn't. Trudy dropped her hand from his face.

"I wasn't ready. I had no idea how fucked it was. It was lonely and loud; dudes were always banging their cells, screaming from that four-by-six box. I hated the blackness of 'lights out.' All those roaches and sick food." Ray Ray threw a rock toward the gutter.

"Damn." Trudy didn't know what to say. She wanted to touch him again but kept her hand at her side.

"I don't want to talk about the shit. That shit made me sick."

But Ray Ray did talk. He was just like a faucet. All the words just gushed out like water.

"Norco separated the prison based on the amount of time served. The hard dudes were all housed at the top. Those were your murderers, multiple rapists and crazies. People doing triple-life and shit. The middle levels held the felons, one-time killers and drug dealers. The lower lev-els, where I was, were all recently popped. Car thieves, small-time crooks, domestic violence stuff. All of them down there were doing short time, anything six years or less."

But in California, the prison population had quadrupled overnight, thanks to the new "Three Strikes You're Out." Jails were brimming. Prisons had filled to capacity. Some facilities resorted to using old army barracks to deal with the mad overcrowding.

"I remember them first few months at Norco. They housed me and the other guys in a large abandoned army barrack. That old barrack was huge, with bunk beds squashed together. Looked like a Boy Scout lodge, if you didn't look close. But we had windows you could see through. There was a grassy area with trees. I'd watch birds and squirrels play all the time."

Ray Ray remembered their early-morning chirps. He'd wake up, keep his eyes shut, lay there and listen. With his eyes closed, he would pretend he wasn't in prison anymore. Free from bars and the wild, hellish nightmares inside.

"In Norco, the Mexicans and blacks had a war going on. As soon as I got in, a Mexican bashed in my face. Another one caught me and broke my left thumb. But the guard was a brother and had one guy transferred. The other one bunked two beds down the way. I waited half the night working the good hand I had. I ripped a piece of metal from under the bunk. I sanded it back and forth on the rough redbrick floor. I crawled to the guy's bed on my hands and my knees and jammed the metal piece in his eye. Everybody heard that Mexican guy scream. They took his ass out on a stretcher."

Trudy winced, but Ray Ray kept talking.

"But, man, that barrack shit didn't last long. One of the inmates tried to escape. There was a mad gunshot hunt that lasted five days. The whole place was flashlights and bloodhounds. But they got him. Found the man way down the interstate, panting underneath an old Monte Carlo. The next day they hacked all those tall redwoods down. Bulldozers came and killed all the bushes and grass. The guards said it impeded their ability to see. The next thing I knew, the whole place was concrete. The birds were all gone and there was nothing outside except barbed wire and chain-link for miles. The nightmares came then. And the constant fighting for your life. I didn't think I could make it." Ray Ray shook his head but looked up and smiled.

"But that's when I got your first letter."

Trudy couldn't help but smile back at Ray Ray. She and Ray Ray went back. Ever since the eighth grade. He was a knucklehead even back then. If he wasn't reading, Ray Ray was doing something to get her attention. Always giving her things. Ballpoints, big giant Frito-Lay bags, Snickers and Milky Way bars by the fistfuls, and wallets with other people's I.D. His candy-bar skin had the prettiest dimples. Flashed her his naughty-boy smile whenever he got caught.

Back in the day, Ray Ray's whole family was crazy. All six of 'em shoved in this one-bedroom unit. Mashed in there like some rats. His daddy drove semis, was gone half the time. Nobody was home to control 'em. One brother was gang-banging; another sold crack. Their mama loved to sit in the car with her daughter and talk shit all day and smoke weed. But the streets took a toll on Ray Ray's whole family. His father fell asleep at the wheel one night and died. One brother was found knifed in a vacant apartment. The other brother got popped and was doing back-to-back life. His oldest sister OD'd on a bad batch of smack. Ray Ray's apartment, which had always been the loudest part of the street, was as quiet and still as a morgue. They were all gone, everybody, except for his mama, who sat up all day like a zombie. But Ray Ray took care of her. Brushed her thin hair and cooked all her food. Some fools might have left. Couldn't deal with the trouble. But Ray Ray stood by. He took care of his mother. Trudy had always admired that about him.

But she knew he was wild. Completely un-tamed and totally street. With that burn on his cheek, he was still super fine. Crazy and sexy as hell.

"Thanks for getting those guys off me," Trudy said, clutching her purse to her chest.

"No problem," Ray Ray said, averting his eyes.

146

He could feel the mild warmth from her bronze, even skin.

Trudy shyly let her braids fall into her face. "So how you been doin'? How's it feel to be out?" Trudy could feel the warm-oven pull too.

"Feels like I don't never want to go back!"

"I heard that," Trudy said. It felt good being with Ray Ray. With him she could be her natural free self. He was easy and clear as cool water.

"How's your mother gettin' along?" Trudy wanted to know.

"Same ol' same ol'," Ray Ray told her. "Moms and me still kickin' it. We doing our best to stay up." Ray Ray flashed her one of his rarely seen smiles. "I appreciate you stopping by to see her sometimes. That meant a lot to me, girl."

When Trudy smiled back, Ray Ray's whole body throbbed. He strained against the strong urge to grab her and kiss her. But Trudy used to be Lil Steve's woman. Lil Steve was his friend. It meant she was off-limits. So he held in his feelings. Kept his emotions in check. He stayed as cool as a Canadian lake. In prison, you learn quick not to show your emotions. If you did, those fools used them against you.

"You tell me if anybody messes with you, girl," Ray Ray said with a hint of mad dog in his eyes. But when he looked in her face, his hard eyes went soft. His thick lashes fluttered back toward the ground.

"I will," Trudy said, looking away. She could feel the soft pull of his eyes on her back. But Trudy knew how to cover her emotions too. She could be as calm as a mannequined window.

"Just lay low, Ray Ray. You're out, so be cool. Don't do anything dumb. And stay the fuck away from that fool Lil Steve."

"Lil Steve's all right. You know that's my boy."

"He's a punk," Trudy shot back.

Ray Ray threw another rock to the other side of the street. He never liked that Trudy was with Lil Steve. It cut him. It tore the pink meat of his soul.

"Why you so worried about me and Lil Steve?" Ray Ray asked sharply. He studied Trudy's face. "At one time you had no problem dealing with blood," Ray Ray reminded her.

"Dealing with him was the worst thing I did in my life. I didn't know how jacked he could be."

"So you deal with folks before you know who they are? And the ones that you been knowing for years, those the ones you choose to leave alone." Ray Ray was smart. He was trying to trip her up. All he ever wanted was for her to want him.

"Lil Steve's so to the curb. You don't need to hang with him. Damn, Ray Ray, he lives in his car. Homeboy ain't going nowhere but down."

"Shit, many a fool's a paycheck from living in a car. Shoot, if Tony don't cut me my paycheck soon, I could be out there myself."

"But he doesn't care where he is, Ray Ray," Trudy pleaded.

"And where are you going, girl?" Ray Ray wanted to know.

"I'm leaving. I'm getting out this skank town."

"That's why you doing this bank job with him?"

Damn, Trudy thought, he already knows. Lil Steve is obviously planning to use him.

"Ray Ray, don't trip! He can handle it himself."

"You got to have two. It's a two-man job, baby. One hits and one drives the car."

Trudy stared at the brown summer lawn, squeezing her braids in her hand.

"Why you acting so scared? You didn't used to trip like this." Ray Ray pulled some of her braids with his fingers. "You used to be fearless. A one-woman bullet. We used to clean up at Fedco, back in the day. You sure there ain't something you want to say?"

Trudy was stuck. How could she tell him she was setting Lil Steve up without blowing the whole fucking scam?

Ray Ray had his doubts, so he just put it out there.

"Why you doing this, huh? Why'd you pick Lil Steve?"

Ray Ray was suspicious. She had to say something quick to make him believe she was on the up-and-up.

"Look, Ray Ray. All I'm trying to do is protect you. You just got out. You need to walk a straight line. The only reason I picked Lil Steve is because he's the best. Of all the players in town, he's never been popped. Even white people like him. They don't even look at him twice. Shoot, the brother is as smooth as a kindergarten slide. I'm just doing this one thing so I can pack up and step. All I'm saying is just watch your back, okay?"

"Lil Steve's my homie, nigga been had my back. Besides," he said, playing with a handful of her braids, "I'll walk a straight line as soon as you do." Ray Ray mildly touched a few soft fingers of her hand but Trudy gently pulled them away.

"You need a ride?"

"Naw, I'll be okay."

Ray Ray watched her thunderous strut down the street. In no time she was at the end of the block. But she stopped and looked back when she got to the corner. She stood there for a moment, holding his gaze, before slowly turning the corner. He noticed one of Trudy's long braids lying on the ground. He picked it up, fingering its length. The knotted end held a tiny smooth shell. Ray Ray shoved the braid deep inside the well of his pocket. Some folks you never get over.

# 12

## Trudy and Lil Steve

Trudy had a smile on her face after seeing Ray Ray that day. She came home, peeled off her dress, left it there on the floor and tossed her snagged nylons in the tall kitchen trash.

Billie Holiday sang from the transistor in the corner.

Her apartment was small but it glowed from assorted candles. She had an old couch with a king-sized sheet hiding the ripped stuffing. There were artwork and beautiful coffee table books, small statues and hand-painted ashtrays and bowls. Almost everything in there was stolen. The outside of her apartment might be covered in bars, but the inside looked like a museum.

But the smashed–beer can life was right outside her door. Wild cursing and gunshots leaked under each screen. Trudy crushed a cockroach with her shoe.

Trudy had wanted to hit the tan-suit man for a while. Had watched his balance shoot up fifty grand in two weeks. The man put twenty-five grand in every week like clockwork. He was as regular as the *L.A. Times.*

She remembered the first time she'd seen him pull into the lot. He drove a spanking-new Lexus, an LS400, one of the best-rated cars in the world. It had a moonroof and beautiful tan leather seats and drove so quiet it must have felt like riding on air. That's what Trudy wanted. Real long money. Not to just look like she had some, like her mother. Not to have to check the price tag of every damn thing she picked up. She was sick of counting every red cent every time she got it. Sick of penny-ante schemes that brought in a few bucks. Trudy wanted real money so she could finally get out. She wanted to get away from all those reaching and touching men. All the long, knowing looks as she walked down the street. Even at work, that mess didn't stop.

Once this white teller reached over and yanked a fistful of her braids.

"Wow," he said, smiling. "I just had to touch 'em. I was wondering what they felt like."

Well, Trudy would have let him feel her hand whack his pink cheek but the big boss happened to walk in right then.

Trudy got smart after that happened. She learned to flash folks a cold, evil eye. People left her alone then. They didn't talk to her at all. Oh, she knew they thought she was stuck-up, had some chip on her shoulder, called her a "nigga bitch" and shit behind her back. But so what? Shoot, she didn't care. Trudy would stop in her tracks, flip a hard, crowbar stare, and most folks left her alone.

All Trudy wanted now was one final haul. At twenty, she was perfectly content at being alone. A nice, fantastic heist could get her way far away. Big money could buy her a brand new address. A newly paved place on a clean, tree-lined street. No more "Trudy with the booty" thrown up in her face. No more heels snapping off as she walked down the block. No more men trying to touch her or fondle her breasts. She hated the cracked, filthy streets and those helicopter nights and the wild screams of sirens going off all the time and bums always begging for money. New clothes didn't feel good walking up the same broken-down steps. One giant haul was all Trudy wanted. And to finally pay Lil Steve back.

Trudy had learned lots of schemes while working at the club. Car thieves and men doing repo-man scams, or chicks passing bad checks in stores. While working at the bank you always heard stories too. Her all-time favorite was Donali. Donali came to work wearing Prada or Armani and drove a cute white convertible Jag. Of course, he shouldn't have done that because that's how they got him. His salary didn't cover that shit. But his scam was unique and didn't take much effort. See, Donali used to switch the signature cards. His friend would come in and make great big withdrawals, and since Donali switched the cards his friend's signature always matched. For months they ran that scam, making off with large dollars, but the nice car and clothes got the camera pointed on him. The next thing Trudy knew they were taking him out in cuffs.

But Trudy had a plan that removed her completely. That's where the tan-suit man came in. Oh, there were others but he seemed the most reliable. Always friendly. Always her line. Always the same big deposit. That's why Trudy got the job at the bank in the first place. She didn't want to rob the bank. She wasn't a fool. She didn't want to end up like Donali's dumb ass. No, the bank was the place to find out who had money. To the dime, she knew exactly how much people had.

After watching the tan-suit man for months, Trudy went to the DMV. It was right after the tan-suit man made his eight large deposits. She spotted an older male clerk working off in a corner. Trudy waited in his line. When she got to the front she unbuttoned her top button. Her cleavage rested right on the ledge. "Excuse me," she said, making her voice sound troubled. She wiped her eyelash for effect.

"Are you okay? What's the matter with you, sugar?" The clerk got real close to Trudy's face. And although he tried hard to watch her pitiful eyes, he stayed latched to the deep wedge in her chest.

"This chick tripped out and keyed up my ride."

The man gave Trudy a fatherly nod. "You best not fool with them married ones, honey." He heard stories like this all the time.

"He's not married. His ex was just crazy. That skank followed me all the way to my house. Poured nail polish all over my brand-new waxed paint and deflated all four of my Pirellis."

"Well, call the police, honey. They'll put her in line." His thumb wanted to rub Trudy's skin.

Trudy started to pout. She batted her lashes. She leaned down to show the deep meat of her cleavage and stuck out her glossed bottom lip.

"I don't have anything. I just have her plate numbers."

"Well, give them to me, honey. We'll catch that heifer. I had a few hellions trying to ruin my life once. I'd be happy to get one off the street."

Worked like a charm. He was eager to help her. He gave Trudy the name, address and phone number of the car. He gave Trudy his phone number too.

"Be safe, young thang," he said to her as she left. "Give me a call if you just want to talk." The man said it like talking was the last thing on his mind. He smoothed his tie over the arch of his stomach as she left.

Trudy drove to the tan-suit man's house in Beverly Hills.

She had to park a block away so she wouldn't be seen. She let her seat fall all the way back so she was lying flat and looking out of her side-views. She saw the man go into a large gated mansion. Two men followed him back out to his car. One of them was a brother in a black SUV. The tan-suit man handed him a large manila envelope. Another man popped open the trunk and laid a plastic bag inside the tire. The tan-suit man got in his car and took off. The black SUV took off too.

Dealers, she thought. Just what I figured.

Trudy lifted her seat back up and switched on the ignition. She thought for a long time on the lonely ride home.

"Dealers. How do you hit dealers? How do you get that long cash and not get caught?"

Then it hit her. You don't. You get some dumb lowlife fool to do the shit for you.

When Trudy got home, she dialed Lil Steve's bootleg cell phone.

"You busy?"

"Trudy with the booty? Girl, is that you?"

Trudy cringed, holding the phone slightly away from her ear. She hated being called that.

Lil Steve didn't notice the silence on the other end. He clicked the volume down on his portable TV and popped the seat up in his car.

"Damn, baby, how did I get so lucky?" His legs were spread wider than a hawk's wings in flight, and his hand massaged the seam of his jeans.

He couldn't believe Trudy had called him. She didn't speak to him last week when he saw her outside Dee's. In fact, he didn't think she'd ever speak to him in life.

Lil Steve popped a forty-ounce from the ice chest in the backseat. He sure was enjoying this moment. "So how ya doin'? How's Tony treating you at the club? That clown still won't let me come in."

Trudy didn't want to talk about that. She wanted to get down to business. She knew Lil Steve was interested now. Vernita had casually planted the seed the other day at her shop. Lil Steve had come in to boost some hot roller sets, and Vernita had ended up giving Lil Steve an earful of information, as well as a touch-up and trim.

"Yeah, your girl spilled her guts. Man, that chick can't hold water. Telling her is like passing out flyers." Lil Steve thought he'd wiggled the information from Vernita. He didn't know she was setting him up.

Trudy dipped the tiny brush inside the bright bottle of polish. She slowly stroked each toe an ambulance red.

"Hey, I'm sorry to hear about your mother." Lil Steve's mother had passed last year. Her death was a shock to them all.

"Yeah, life's fucked up," he said, staring at the split in his dashboard. A panhandler worked his way toward Lil Steve's fender. Lil Steve held a gun out of his window. The panhandler jumped back and fell off the curb. "Seems like we got that in common," he said.

"But it doesn't have to be. Not if we focus." Lil Steve leaned up farther in his seat.

"I got my eyes on bigger prizes," Trudy said.

"Does the prize got to do with your job at the bank?"

Trudy smiled and poured herself some more Alize. Lil Steve always thought fast.

"I got a little something something I think we can work on."

Lil Steve thought Trudy was trying to be cute. He always thought he'd taught Trudy how to steal. Took pride in the fact. Like she was his protégé and whatnot.

"I really need your help to pull this thing off. And it's easy. You can do the whole thing alone." What she really wanted to say was please don't use Ray Ray. But Trudy couldn't risk Lil Steve being suspicious.

"Look, if we do this, you and me split it fifty-

fifty." Trudy knew that Lil Steve would be holding all the money. She reminded him why he needed to give her a share.

"And remember, there's the security tape at the bank. You don't want to give me a reason to go canary. You're way too pretty for jail." Trudy sugared her voice, stroking the hairs of his ego. Trudy knew which side her bread was buttered on. If you want a man's help, you got to give him his props. "You're the best, Lil Steve. I need you to make this work. You're the first person I thought of," she said.

"So you want me, huh, baby?" Lil Steve asked, smiling. He held the cell phone real close to his mouth. His hand rubbed the inseam of his jeans once again.

"Oh, I want it." Trudy let that sink in too. She wanted Lil Steve to focus on that. She had to make him think that she wanted him too.

Trudy poured a glass of Alize and sang along with Billy . . .

*"God bless the child that's got his own."*

# 13

## Charles and Tony

The next day Charles went to gamble at Dee's. "Come on, double six. Come home to Daddy." A man held the dice tightly in his fist. He brought the two dice right up to his lips. He blew on them slow, then shook them both wildly, tossing them with all his might, and let go.

"Woowee! That's what I'm talking about." The double six paid the man thirty-to-one. His ten bucks turned into three hundred.

"Gimme a double tray, the hard way, y'all hush yo' mouths." The man rattled the dice in his hands. "If I hit this bitch, all y'all drink free."

Charles watched the man like he was transfixed. Everything the man called came up. But Charles wasn't ready. He held a fistful of bills.

"I'ma let this ride," the winning man said. "I can feel my point coming in again."

The man looked at Charles. "Don't be skeerd, boy! You best get in this game and make some money in here, son. Lady Luck is red-hot tonight!"

Charles put his crumpled stack of bills on the table. He placed it down like he didn't want to let it go.

"Hey, cue ball!" The man laughed at Tony's bald head. "I'ma take your ends and make some for your poot-butt friend too."

What Charles didn't know was this game was fixed. The big man and Tony had a system working against Charles. They let him win a few bucks just to keep him playing, but there was no way he'd ever win big.

"You putting all that down, son?" Tony asked Charles, examining the stack of bent twenties.

"Shoot, you know that's the only way to make serious money." The man with the dice winked knowingly at Charles. Charles smiled meekly back. He needed to win. He had to recover his losses. He'd dug a deep hole with Tony already. Luckily for him Tony hadn't sweated him yet.

Charles studied the man holding the lacquered red dice. The man was so lucky. Won boo-coo chips already. A thick stack of bills sat at the man's waist. Charles carefully placed his wager on him.

"You hot today," Tony said, pouring the man more scotch.

It was three o'clock and Charles was gambling on his lunch break again.

The man grabbed his suspenders. He stood wide-legged and grinned. "I'm just a squirrel in your world, trying to get me a nut. Now stand back and watch me work magic."

"Well, go 'head," Tony said. "Shoot your best shot."

The man threw the dice toward the back of the table. The dice rolled over the dark fabric and dropped. Both red squares added up to seven.

"Oh well," Tony said, quickly raking in the money. He raked all of Charles's cash too.

The man with the suspenders grabbed his bill-fold and hat. "Luck's just like a parking meter, son. You better get before your ticker runs out." The man smacked Charles real hard on the back. "Tony!" he roared before walking down toward the door. He handed Tony some bills as his cigar smoke lingered in the room. "Until you're better paid," the man said.

Charles had been gambling heavily for at least three weeks straight. Each check he brought home was smaller than the next. There was no use stalling around anymore. He owed seven grand now. He was going to have to get the money he had saved at the bank.

He picked up his leather mail carrier's sack and walked back out to his truck. He always bought a pint at the liquor store on Stocker. It was way off his route and no one would spot him. He put on a long coat to hide the uniform he wore; he couldn't risk some damn snitch turning him in.

Trudy followed Charles to the liquor store and waited for him to come out. She watched his reflection in the liquor store door. Charles was caught at the light right there off Stocker. She had just palmed some gum at the Liquor Barn on the corner, and even though the light had already changed, Trudy rushed out against the flashing red hand so she could cross right in front of his truck. That's why she threw an extra bounce in her step. She wanted to bait him. Reel him in. Give him something to make his mouth water.

When Trudy stepped off the curb, she swung her wide hips. She pulled down her V-neck and thrust out her breasts. Immediately horns started to bark.

"Damn," Charles said out loud to himself. He slammed on his brakes and made a U-turn into the mall.

Trudy glimpsed his broad frame in the mall's store windows. Charles was fine and linebacker wide.

Trudy remembered what Vernita told her one day.

"Girl, you ain't had no love until you had

wide-man love." Vernita had licked the chocolate icing off her fork. "Lay on 'em just like a futon. Put your drink right in their shoulder blade, honey." Vernita smacked the chocolate from her tongue.

Trudy planted herself near the mirrored perfume counter. That was always the first thing you saw in a store. Trudy wanted to be easy to spot.

"Trudy with the booty," Charles mouthed under his breath.

Trudy pretended to examine the Lancôme lipstick.

"You like that shade?" Charles asked, pressing up.

Trudy twirled the burgundy tube until the dark lipstick slid up. She didn't even look at Charles at all. She gently stroked the tip back and forth across her lips and then carefully smoothed the burgundy all over her full mouth.

Charles stood mesmerized. This was one sexy freak. He waved the salesman over.

"Could you please ring this up for the lady?" Charles asked.

The salesman was a little swish with dark walnut eyes. He boldly gazed over Charles's wide brick-wall body. "Man-oh-man," he mumbled under his breath.

"Thank you," Trudy said. "But you didn't have to do that."

"I wanted to," he said, pulling out his credit

card, hoping the small purchase would go through. He sighed, relieved when the salesman came back.

Trudy smiled at Charles. But he didn't know what to say. "You sing at Dee's, don't you?"

"Yeah," Trudy said. "But I work at a bank. Singing is just my side gig."

Trudy's warm smile made him tingle in his thighs.

"I wanted to talk to you for a minute." Trudy rubbed her lips together. "I hope you don't think I'm out of line."

Charles felt flattered. He couldn't believe she was talking to him. He let his mail sack slip to the floor. He carried his bag in case a co-worker saw him. He could always say he was delivering a package.

"I saw your girl at the bank this past Friday."

"My girl." Charles hadn't told her about Flo.

Trudy saw the question marks flash in his eyes. "Look, I don't know her, know her. She gets her hair done at the same salon. I've seen you guys out a couple of times."

Charles just waited. He didn't know what was coming.

"She came in today. She got in my line," Trudy continued.

Charles immediately became concerned. His eyes darted around the store. He was nervous and quickly hiked his bag up his back. It was four o'clock and technically, he was still on the job; a co-worker might turn him in.

"I'd like to talk to you about it alone if I could," Trudy said. "Do you have a card?"

Charles didn't want her calling him at home. Flo might pick up the phone. And even though he'd never owned a business card in his life, he peered in his wallet like he did.

"Looks like I ran out," he said sheepishly, digging both hands in his pockets.

"Here." Trudy handed him a matchbook from Dee's. "I'll be there tonight. I go on at nine. Maybe you and I could talk later."

Charles gently touched her fingers as he took the book of matches. "I guess I'll just wait until then."

Trudy waved and gave him one last farewell wiggle, making her way to the escalator upstairs. She felt great. Charles was just who she wanted. Everything was turning out fine. She felt so good she didn't even steal the pair of silver earrings she'd hidden in her hand the whole time. The earrings had turned her left hand into slime. She placed them down in the shoe section and left.

Charles went back to work and finished his shift. He couldn't wait to get back to Dee's Parlor that night. He asked for another advance on his check.

"That's your last one," his supervisor told him, annoyed.

But Charles didn't care if his money ran thin. Tonight he was going to meet Trudy at Dee's. Trudy with the booty wanted to meet up with him! The sun roared against his white teeth.

# 14

## Charles and Flo

"What, you're not going to talk anymore?" Flo asked. It had been ten tense days since Charles had tossed that bottle.

Charles yanked a beer from the refrigerator door. He drank it while watching T.V. It was night but it was hotter in the house than outside.

Flo was nervous about Charles finding out about the car.

She secretly parked the car around the corner and walked so Charles wouldn't see the car when he got home.

When Flo stood right in front of the set, Charles went back into the kitchen.

"How long you going to be mad?" Flo asked him direct.

"I ain't mad," Charles said.

"Yes, you are," Flo shot back. She tried to touch his arm but Charles snatched it away.

Charles avoided Flo's eyes and swallowed more beer, squeezing the cold bottle in his hand.

Charles walked from the room, took off his clothes and got in the shower.

Flo quietly sat on the living room couch. She heard the beating of water. She flipped through a few channels, got bored and turned it off, and walked back into the kitchen to check the stove.

Flo had rushed home so she could beat Charles from work. She had hurried home to make a huge dinner for Charles. Cooked everything he liked. Cabbage, meatloaf, mashed potatoes and gravy. Kind of a peace offering for the sour week they'd had. For the nine days she'd had the car Flo felt nothing but guilt. She was sad about spending all their money and even tried to give the car back.

"Sorry," the dealer said. He told her it was too late. "Once the wheels leave the lot, lady, it's yours," the man yapped.

Flo wanted to tell Charles about the car but it was never the right time. Since she didn't want him to find out by seeing the car in the driveway, Flo pretended to ride the bus and parked the car around the block.

Flo stopped mashing the potatoes and watched Charles get dressed.

Charles and she hadn't been speaking much

lately. They mumbled the occasional "pass me the salt" or "did anyone call?" Just your day-to-day small talk.

She wondered how long he was going to stay mad. Flo couldn't stand this horrible dry silence. She wanted to start over. Start the weekend off right. Have him be sweet to her again. She didn't know if Charles knew if she bought the car or not. If he did, he didn't say. But she knew she'd fucked up by spending all their money. The dream of owning a home was completely gone now. Flo mashed the potatoes with passion.

Charles got out of the shower and tied the towel around his waist. The water rolling down his glistening calves made a small puddle on the wood floor. Dripping a trail to the bedroom, he stood at the door of the closet, thumbing through all his good shirts. Those were the ones he wore when he went out. They still had the dry cleaner's plastic around them.

Flo sat quietly. Her eyes searched his back. She watched him take out the pressed shirt from the plastic. Watched him squeeze the baby oil and rub it over his firm body. He looked at his triceps in the mirror a long time and flexed before putting on his shirt.

Charles walked back to the bathroom again. Flo's eyes followed his skin.

Charles couldn't wait to get out the house tonight. He sprayed a heavy layer of cologne against his throat. When he caught Flo looking at him in the mirror, he closed the bathroom door with his foot.

"Damn," Charles said, blowing a kiss to himself. "You definitely one fine-looking brotha!" Charles clicked the bathroom light off and walked toward the living room mantel. He couldn't wait to get to the club and see Trudy tonight. He took his car keys out of his pocket.

It was one of those hot, blazing L.A. nights. So hot you had to drag out those cheap metal fans and run them full blast. Yank all the shades down to keep the cool in. Keep your freezer stacked full of ice trays. And even after that, the dead heat crept in just the same. But the funny thing was, no matter how hot it got in each room in their apartment, it sure was chilly between Flo and Charles.

Lately all Charles wanted to do was get out the house. He came home later and later from work and as soon as he did, he was itching to get to Dee's.

Flo sat down again on the couch. She hadn't been feeling so well lately; must be some nasty bug. She had cooked all that food but didn't want to eat. She clicked the TV on, nestling one hand inside a bag of Doritos. The bag made a horrible rustling sound every time her hand jabbed inside.

Charles's black shoes sounded extra loud on the hardwood floors. He carefully buttoned the front of his shirt and then picked up his wallet.

"You're not going out again?" Flo asked.

Charles didn't speak. He picked up his brush and stood by the mantel, smoothing his short hairs back down.

"I thought maybe we'd spend some time together tonight, go see a movie or something," Flo said. "I made all this food. You ain't even going to eat?"

Charles kept brushing away at his hair. He felt an urgency to leave. Trudy was waiting for him already.

Flo tried again, tried to sound more upbeat. "That scary movie looks good. You like scary movies. Maybe we could go and see that?"

Charles pulled his black sports coat from the closet.

Flo tried harder. "You know Freeman's in it. I know you like him. We could go to the eight o'clock show." Flo tried to kiss his shoulder but Charles pulled away. He shoved his wallet inside his back pocket.

"Well, go on then," Flo said. "Just see if I'm home." Flo sloshed more Coke down her throat.

Charles smiled to himself after Flo spoke. Yeah, she'd be home wearing her scrunchy pink curlers. Her robe riding over her large stretchmarked stomach, sound asleep, snoring loud on the couch.

Flo couldn't understand why Charles was being so hard. They usually made good love after those horrible brawls.

Flo and Charles would lie side by side like two old junk cars. And then one of them would roll or turn over sudden. And she'd touch his flesh, feeling his warm, juicy skin. Then the room would heat up like a fierce, roaring engine. Like a hot match against the black asphalt. He'd seize Flo and she'd please him any way he wanted. Charles would tug her warm frame hungrily, sucking her neck. Licking and pawing and gnawing her body until the deep moans escaped from her throat. Entering her so fast, so urgent and deep that Flo didn't have the chance to get up sometimes. And her diaphragm sat on the cold tile smiling. Waiting inside the pink case. But Flo couldn't stop the rocket fuel heat. She couldn't ignore her body's aching need. The wild, seething need to hold on to something. Hold tight even while her entire world sank. Even though a dark sadness had lodged in her body. A sadness that clamped down and wouldn't let go. Seemed like the only time she felt alive was when they were fighting like dogs. Clawing and gnawing away at each other. Trying to feel something while sinking in sand. They only got close after horrible drama. After chairs were knocked down and clothes were snatched off. Scratching for something that slipped away each day. But just like those gray, heavy waves at the beach, one minute you're up to your ankles in wet and the next you're just standing in sand.

See, Charles and Flo had hit a dry season. After Charles's affair, Flo began holding back on sex. She wanted to take something. Something to really make him suffer. So she slept on the narrow, slim edge of their bed. She lay breathing hard under the single tight sheet. She lay rigid, never letting a leg bend or arm dangle over to his side. She wanted to teach him. Keep his body near starving. And Flo, who'd always worn nightgowns to bed, began to sleep naked to torture him more. She'd stroke her own body, left one hand between her legs, but she never touched Charles's waiting flesh.

But now Flo was the one who waited hour after hour. She wanted Charles to seize her but he never turned her way. When she finally reached for him, Charles let out a snore. When her fingers grazed his biceps he jerked back his arm. When she tried to spoon his skin he refused to roll over. Eventually, Flo stopped trying. She lay quiet on the sheet, while Charles quietly pleased himself.

There was nothing worse, Flo thought, staring at the chipped rotting ceiling. There was nothing like lying right next to your man. Nothing like wanting him, wanting him to reach out and touch you. Having him so close you can feel his warm, steamy skin. Lying there blazing under sizzling covers, listening to your own violent, lonely heart scream. Being so close, so damn close to the one thing you wanted and not being able to touch it.

Flo got up and threw some cold water over her face.

No, Flo didn't know where she and Charles had lost it. But as sure as she was standing barefoot on the floor, she knew sure as hell it was gone.

"There's got to be someone," Flo thought to herself. She paced back and forth across cold bathroom tile. "There's no way he can lay day after day and not touch me." Flo splashed some more water, which ran down to her toe. "There's got to be somebody else."

# 15

## Ray Ray and Charles

"Look-a here, look-a here." Big Percy tapped Ray Ray's shirt. Trudy walked to the front door after singing the first set. Vernita was supposed to meet her at ten.

Big Percy smiled his sloppy-mouth grin. Even though Trudy had been working at Dee's for months, Big Percy stayed up in her face.

"Well, if it ain't Trudy with the booty," Percy said, blocking her path. "Bet that ass tastes just like a Hershey's."

Trudy rolled her eyes and just kept on walking. A bum hit her up before she got to her car. She jabbed a few bucks in his hand.

"God bless you." The bum smiled from his black, deep-grooved face. Trudy smiled but kept walking. Her Honda was parked in the dark lot. She opened the hood and quickly unhooked the cables. She shut it and walked back toward the club's door.

Percy's eyes ran up and down Trudy's body. "So, you too good now, huh? Can't talk to a brother proper?" Percy talked with the thick lisping tongue of a man who'd lost all his front teeth. He stood over Trudy like a solid brick wall. He was six feet and almost as wide.

"Could you back the fuck up?" Trudy said, irritated. She waved when she saw Vernita coming up the walk but Big Percy still blocked her path.

"Ohhh, well excuse me, queen!" Big Percy said mockingly. "Ain't this about a bitch. Ass all on Front Street, spread all over the whole damn town and we got the nerve to act uppity."

Vernita popped her gum but didn't say a thing. She'd been doing hair all day and wanted a drink. "Come on, Percy, I'm thirsty. Just let me in and quit trippin'."

"Oh, hello, ofay lover," Big Percy turned toward her. "Still sucking the white man's dick?"

Vernita had dated Carlos a little while back. He was half Mexican and Chinese but Big Percy didn't care. To him anybody nonblack was white.

"And who do you think's on the other end of that welfare dick yo' mama's been sucking ever since yo' ass been old enough to hold a food stamp?" Trudy snapped back.

\* \* \*

Ray Ray came from the black drape and smiled at Trudy. Homegirl sure was something. Percy was glaring down her throat but Trudy still didn't care. She looked like she'd whup him right there like his mama.

"Be cool, man," Ray Ray said, watching Trudy's hot eyes. "Come on, man, let 'em come through."

Trudy kept her head straight and walked in strong and tall. She couldn't stand Percy. He had an ignorant side. His overgrown body and dead, eaten-out mouth looked like something you dragged out for Halloween. He was always tasting himself too. Sucking his own lips and wagging his tongue, which was real long and rough and always hung out, like you best watch your young boys around his big nasty ass.

But Trudy couldn't help but smile back at Ray Ray. She could feel that soft pull weight against her back.

"I'm glad you never stooped low to go with that brother," Vernita whispered to her once they both got inside.

Trudy didn't say anything. She'd always liked Ray Ray. If he hadn't grown up in a house so damn crazy, things might have turned out different for them.

"A woman like you could have straightened my ass out," Ray Ray used to tell her all the time. But some things were so crooked you couldn't get 'em straight. All that stabbing and stealing.

All them hoodlums with guns. All the cocaine and heroin and crackheads strung out. All them 'hoish type women who hovered near his door—shoot, Ray Ray's road was mapped out.

Ray Ray leaned against his old tailpipe-dragging Lincoln, blowing low trails of smoke from his Newport. His dark, rusty skin glowed under the moon. The right side of his face was totally smooth; the left side was ravaged with scars. The burn mark resembled a slab of grilled ribs, left too long on the flame. Ray Ray scratched the burnt side of his face.

He walked inside Dee's and fed ten quarters into the cigarette machine and waited for the green and white box to drop out. He lit a cigarette and scanned the smoky, dim room. Charles was sitting at a small table near the wall. He was talking with Tony. Ray Ray opened the pack and walked over.

"Whatchu say, Ray Ray?" Tony's upper lip rose way over his gums. His wet smile was glistening with spit.

"You got the winning hand," Ray Ray said, rubbing the huge scar on his face. He walked close to Tony and got near his face. "Man, I been here over three and a half weeks. When I'm s'posed to get paid?"

"Boy, please, don't be bothering me tonight. The fight's in a few days and I got a lot on my plate."

Ray Ray stayed by his side, kept clocking his back until Tony stopped in his tracks. "Jailbird like you is lucky to get any work. You'll get paid whenever I say." Tony lit a half-smoked Winston, daring Ray Ray to comment, then boldly walked back toward the kitchen.

Charles smiled when he saw Ray Ray come into the room. Ray Ray was one cocky, cold-blooded fool. Charles was older, but he remembered him from high school.

"Zap'nin," Ray Ray mumbled to Charles. Ray Ray was fuming because Tony had given him the runaround again. "That overseer nigga. I ought to kick his fat ass." He turned around and gave Charles a pound.

"Man, I'm glad you came and sat next to me. I'm dodging Tony myself. I owe that sucka some money."

"You owe that fool and the nigga owes me. How much you in the hole for?"

"Seventy-nine hundred." Charles took a large gulp from his drink. His eyes rolled away toward the black, empty stage.

"Damn, man! How you let yo' shit get outta hand?" Ray Ray asked.

"Tony's been letting me gamble on credit," Charles said proudly. He wasn't real worried yet. He smiled in Ray Ray's hard face. "Man, I got money." Charles rubbed his chin, bragging. "If I wanted to, I could write a check for the whole amount now."

"Oh, yeah?" Ray Ray said, chuckling to himself. Charles talked like all of them other small-time gamblers, trying to act like they never needed cash. "Well, I wouldn't borrow none of that punk ass's money. The interest alone is a bitch and a half."

"He don't charge me interest." Charles smiled triumphantly.

"I work for the brother. He charges everyone interest. If he ain't charging you interest, my man, then you must got something his funky butt wants."

Ray Ray was tripping, Charles thought to himself. He was a broke jailbird who didn't own shit. He didn't understand money like him. Charles ordered another beer on credit.

"I guess he just likes me," Charles told Ray Ray proudly.

Ray Ray looked away from Charles's dumb face. "So how's Flo?" Ray Ray asked him. He turned the chair backward and straddled his seat, sprawling his thick thighs open wide. He pulled a sharp blade from the back of his pocket and sliced open a new pack of Doublemint gum.

"I don't know, man. Flo don't move me no more."

"That a fact?" Ray Ray said, scanning the

room, barely listening. He folded the gum over his tongue.

"She's making it really hard for me, man. All I do, all day long, is deliver folks' mail. Working overtime hours so we can get our own place. Get up out that hollow apartment." Charles shook his head. He wanted sympathy from his friend.

Ray Ray pulled on his Newport and held in his smoke, blowing it over Charles's head. Charles had been the same stupid fool since grade six. Never satisfied with shit. Whining about this, crying about that. Eyeballing everything that lay across the street. Thinking everybody's grass was always greener than his. Forgetting both sides had to be mowed. Shoot, where Flo and Charles sat looked like paradise to him. Brother never knew what he had.

"I don't know. I'm thinking of firing Flo, man. All she cares about is herself," Charles said.

"Shit, dog. That's how most people is." Ray Ray stroked the small hairs of his well-groomed goatee. He didn't know why Charles complained all the time. Flo was in-house pussy that could cook and looked sweet. "Don't slip." Ray Ray smiled at his friend. "Another muthafucka be up in there like ice."

"So what? I'm bored with her, man. Used to be she waited for me after work. Used to have on some lipstick, a little perfume too. Now when I come home her hair's all rolled up, nubby legs poking out from her robe. I don't even like being in the same room with her no more. Everything I thought we had changed."

"I guess she don't know what's out here for you, brotha." Ray Ray scanned the dark club. There were only a few women left. One was heavily made-up in a red, garish dress. Two others bulged way over the rims of their stools. And one sat with her head slung over the bar.

"That's what I'm saying, man! Pussy be up in yo' face. Shit, you should see some of them 'hos I get on my route. Half of 'em come to the door with no panties. How you gonna keep yo' nigga from straying all the time if you don't take care of business at home? And I'm huffin' up and down the street all day long, delivering past dues and coupons. Breathing gas fumes and running from wild, unchained dogs. Thinking of ways we can get something decent."

"Dig it."

"All I wanted was a place where my woman's about me and I'm about her. Working together. Like we used to do."

Charles ordered a Tanqueray mixed with sugary lime juice. He gulped almost half of it down.

"Was y'all working together when you fucked the white girl too?" Ray Ray smiled at Charles. "Oh, my bad. I'm sorry about that, man. I don't mean to bring up yo' past." Ray Ray laughed.

"How do you know about that, man? You were locked up back then."

"Brothas in prison know more about the street than y'all. All we did in that bitch was pump iron and talk shit. Some of those O-Gs know Flo. Homegirl still got it poppin'. Brothas will always keep track of nice ass."

Charles ignored Ray Ray and stayed with the story.

"But, man, the worser the fight, the better the pussy. I make her wait so damn long she's ready to hump on my thigh." Charles laughed so hard he choked.

"I feel you, nigga." Ray Ray nodded in his glass.

"Man, sometimes I take her down on all fours."

"Nigga, please." Ray Ray thought Charles was a trip. Half the women he knew liked it like that.

"It's funny," Charles said, more to himself, "it's like she wants it. Like that shit turns her on."

"Probably does."

"It makes me sick, though. It makes me hate her more." Charles sat back, draining the rest of his glass. "No matter how fucked I get, bashing glass and shit, the next thing I know, baby girl's sucking my dick."

"Not all of 'em are like that, dog," Ray Ray told Charles. He didn't like men who put their hands on their women. Punk men like Charles made him sick.

"Aw, nigga, don't trip. I might throw a bottle at Flo, or rip off her dress. But I never really hurt her. At least not on purpose. I never once used my fists."

"Mm-hmm," Ray Ray said, taking a long drag from his Newport. "You gotta be careful. Not all of 'em play." Ray Ray leaned back in his chair and just laughed.

"What?" Charles asked.

"Man, I had this one trick. Now she was a stone freak." Ray Ray looked away from the stage. "But homechick was my regular shit."

"Yeah, so what happened? Where's she at now?" Charles asked.

"Oh man, it was crazy. But that's what I get for messin' around with stone freaks." Ray Ray put his gum inside a napkin. "But a shit-talking bitch has always been my weakness."

Charles couldn't understand Ray Ray sometimes. Why would he want some ol' filthy 'ho? Charles thought Ray Ray was crazy.

"I had this one chick, man. It was tight, all right. Had one of them snappin' pussys. Pi-ya! You put your shit in and that pussy clamped down like a fat rubber band, you understand? Man, I was sprung. Moved in after knowing her one day. Man, I was only in the eleventh grade. I was on and off the street selling nickel bags to get by. Baby just came up on me one night. Big meaty chick with thick legs talking smack." Ray Ray smiled wide. He rubbed his iron-pumped thighs. "Woo shit! Nigga, now you know that's my type. Her pimp had just busted her bottom lip open. Said she was skimmin' off the top. Told me she was, but it wasn't nothing big—nothing none of the other 'hos didn't do. Shoot, every-body in the game got to take care of themselves, right?"

"Right," Charles said, nodding.

"So we move in and play Mom and Pop and apple pie, right? She's selling pussy and I'm slinging 'Caine. Had plenty money all the time. Ate great every night. You know them thick sloppy joes they sell off 63rd? We was eatin' plenty of them and drinking apricot brandy. Man, everything was just gravy."

"You ain't afraid of getting no disease or noth-ing, man? Pussy been in everybody's ass on the street!" Charles looked at Ray Ray, disgusted.

"That's just it, cuz." Ray Ray leaned closer into Charles's face. "That's the whole thang. You got to be clean to be a 'ho. All them 'hos is like that. Get their shit checked like clockwork. All of 'em use condoms. 'Ho's don't go raw no time."

"So what happened to paradise, man?" Charles asked sarcastically. Ray Ray was always telling him some ghettofied story. But his scarred face made him sick. And his back teeth were jacked. Charles wished Ray Ray would get to the point.

"I broke off the leg of the dining room table. All the nails and shit were hanging all out. I clutched that leg like a club. I swung at her once but I missed. I wanted to beat her, but I couldn't. I held that table leg and froze. But the girl freaks out and runs and falls two flights of stairs. She was stuck in a hospital bed at County for months."

"Damn, man! You're lucky she didn't die. They'd have put your ass away for life." Charles opened a pack of gum and took a piece out. "Why would you even mess with a nasty bitch like that?"

"For love, man. I trusted that 'ho. Gave her half of all my cash. Laid up in the cut like a baby." Ray Ray took a deep drag and blew the smoke out real slow. "I would have stayed with that fuckin' freak for life."

"What'd she do?"

"Well, you know I still had a bad wound from a dog bite on a robbery that went bad. Shit never did heal right. Had to go to County all the time to get it checked and guess what?"

"What?"

"The muthafuckas do an AIDS test on my ass."

"An AIDS test for a dog bite?"

"Told me it was routine and shit. Said they checked everybody. So I say, 'all right, okay. Do the shit, right.' But guess what?"

"Naw, man. You lying, dog." Charles looked straight into Ray Ray's burnt face.

"The muthafucka came up positive," Ray Ray whispered low.

"Damn," Charles said, leaning farther back.

"But wait. Trip this, dog." Ray Ray took his pack of gum and shook a stick out.

"So I get home, right? I'm pissin' bullets, see? I know this bitch musta went raw on some dude or showed me some fake-ass medical report, right. So I get home, but I'm cool, right?"

"Right."

"So I ask her."

"What she say?"

"Said she was straight. Said she never went raw no time."

"I said, 'What about us?' She said it was just me. Said she loved me. Asked me why was I tripping out now."

"But, I'm thinking naw, you a lying-ass trick. And I got the paper to prove it, right?"

"Right."

"So she said, 'No baby, you wrong.' She goes to get her paper. Shows me one and a few others too. 'I'm clean, Ray Ray! I been clean, baby. You know I don't mess around.' So she's pleading now, right? Beggin' and shit. But I don't give a fuck, right? Homegirl fucked with my life. Man, you should have seen the hurt in her eyes. She was begging me, 'Please, Ray Ray. Please, baby, don't,' and I'm holding the leg of the table like Willie Mays.

"But I didn't want to hear that shit, okay?" Ray Ray looked out toward Sonny's trio. Sonny was playing a sad black note solo.

"All I thought was this bitch done killed my ass, okay. That AIDS is a mutha on your mind, dog. For real. That shit ain't no muthafuckin' joke. Shit'll eat your whole fuckin' brain up alive." Ray Ray picked at his teeth and put the toothpick behind his ear.

"So what happened?" Charles asked. He knew Ray Ray was crazy but this shit was deep. He couldn't believe what he was saying.

"Man, I took all my shit and moved out that night. But guess what?"

"What?"

"Some undercovers get me while I'm trying to cop. I get sent back for parole violation. So them muthafuckas test me again. Test everybody that's sent up nowadays, dog. They separate all the AIDS folks from them other muthafuckas. They don't want that shit to get outta hand up there, man.

"So they do the test, right? I even tell 'em I have it. I don't care now. I figure I'm half dead all ready. But guess what?"

"What?"

"The shit comes back negative."

"Naw, dog!"

"Man, I even tell the doctor I got it. Beg 'em to do the test again. They do the shit and it's negative again, man. I don't have it. Never did."

"So what's up?"

"The County fucked up. I did thirteen months behind an AIDS test that went bad. Baby showed up in court in a new suit and all her 'ho friends too. Homegirl coulda got an Academy Award for all the boo-hooing she did for that judge, unbuttoning her blouse and showing him those deep ugly scars. But damn, I couldn't even look at her, dog. I never felt so bad, so damn wrong in my life. If I hadn't come at her she never would have taken that fall. Next thing you know, I'm in lockdown. I had some folks on the outside try to talk to her, dog, but she wasn't checking for me. Man, I tried everything to get out. I just wanted to talk to her, tell her I'm sorry. Say I had made a mistake. But I learned the hard way, you just can't go back. Jail gave me a long time to think about that shit. I was fucked up, man. I was totally wrong. Sometimes you cross the line, and love or 'I'm sorry' don't change a damn thing. You can't dog a woman like that and think you can come home. I heard her pimp is still looking for me. I can't even go up in Hollywood no more."

Ray Ray rubbed the huge burn mark with the palm of his hand.

"It was one of her friends threw that lye in my face." Ray Ray lit up a smoke and blew it out toward the bar. The hideous scar rippled from the flame. "I done crossed the line, fool. It's as simple as that. That shit changed me, nigga. I look at life different. You can knock all you want on yesterday's door but that gone bitch will not let you in." Ray Ray stood up and rubbed the cross at his throat. "The only one I trust now is God."

Charles looked at Ray Ray as he walked away.

## WANT SOME

He was so cool in high school. Girls went crazy
for his ass. But you'd never know it by looking at
him today. Half his teeth jacked. Big scar on his
face. He was wearing a suit, but you could see
underneath. Underneath was twenty miles of
bad road.

# 16

## Trudy and Pearl

"You think this dress makes me look fast?" Trudy scrutinized herself in the tall, scratched-up mirror. She'd picked this dress especially to lure in poor Charles. It clung to her, hung on her womanly parts. Like a wet chicken breast dredged in flour.

Vernita was sitting on the dressing room counter, watching Trudy get ready for her set. It was a dingy room with a few stools, a sad row of square mirrors glued to the wall, and a long, wooden, broken-down counter. The counter was filled with ashtrays, curling irons, lipsticks and beads, fake lashes, eye shadow, gobs of foundation, wigs and a big plastic box stuffed with long, colored feathers. The feathers were used when the girls didn't have time to go do their hair or comb a wig out. They just greased their stuff down and picked a few feathers to match their clinging sequined outfits. There were lots of left-over clothes for last-minute changes. You never knew when a button would pop or a zipper might bust or some crazy drunk fool spill some booze on your dress.

"Fast? Girl, please. You worried about fast in this crusty-ass bar? Girl, you better just go on out there and sing to these fools while they still got some loot in their pockets," Vernita told her.

"So we straight?" Trudy asked. "You know what to do?"

"Girl, I done tol' you, I got it."

Vernita grabbed a blond wig and pulled it over her head. "All I got to do is play Miss Anne, huh?" With the blond wig and her freckles, Vernita easily looked white. Vernita held out her hand like it was a gun. "Gimme all yo' big money, man!" Vernita and Trudy broke into peals of laughter but Trudy's smile dropped when they heard the door handle twist. Vernita yanked the wig off just as Pearl pushed her way through the dressing room door.

"Hey, Miss Pearl," Vernita said. "Whatchu know good." And to quickly change the subject she added. "Trudy thinks that dress is too sexy."

Pearl smoothed her shimmering buttercream dress. Although Pearl was the cook, every now and then she raided the stage. "Ain't nothing wrong with showing how the good Lord done blessed you." With that she adjusted one of her massive bra straps, which lifted her big breasts to a cliffhanger point, jiggling against the dress like they just might bounce out and roll onto the floor.

"Come on, honey, let's get out and work. Sonny come in here awhile ago and said the place was packed. Y'all know what Friday means. Paydays and men who had fights with they ladies and a whole lot of pockets full of cash."

Vernita walked out. "I'll see you out there."

Sonny's combo consisted of Sonny on drums, a soft-spoken man with a slurry lisp. He drank Mickie's Big Mouth beer but didn't talk much. Paid too much attention to his red, wavy locks he had done in a slick, gummed-down process. But he was always respectful, called Trudy "miss" all the time. Never once stepped out of line. Then there was Stanley on bass, a skinny young cat who wore slim suits and dark shades. On top of his head sat a white skipper's hat. He said the hat made him look rich. The piano player looked like he could be eighty, a happy dark-skinned man everyone called Mr. Wade.

Trudy came out and held the microphone until Sonny gave her the nod. Then she walked to the center of the stage. Lots of men's chairs rimmed the edge of the platform. They all leaned back in their seats.

Charles couldn't take his eyes off Trudy. Her eyes were always pointing his way. Like the song she sang was for him. Tony came back and leaned in to tell him this old nasty joke, but Charles never heard him; his eyes never left the stage. He shook Tony's arm from his back.

"Damn, man. You act like you ain't never seen her. Booty been all over the town. You don't want to fool around with that heifer. Head's all messed-up already. Her own mama don't have nothing to do with her. Girl's got her ass so high off the ground you'd think she was the Empire State—"

"Wait a minute, man, she's about to sing another one," Charles said, leaning closer to the stage.

Tony sank back and stubbed another Winston in the ashtray.

Truth was, he had tried to hit on Trudy himself, but Pearl had caught him and loud-talked him in the middle of the room.

"Baby girl don't want to mess with no drunk ass like you. She's my niece. She's a singer. You hired her to sing. She ain't one of them boozy sluts you bring up in here. Got to pay most of 'em just to look at yo' ass. You best sit down and keep drinking that cheap liquor you serve and stay out that chile's face." Pearl stood her ground. The whole place got quiet. Trudy was family. Tony was out of line. The bar waited to see what Tony was going to say. But all Tony did was walk out.

"Someday, I'ma hafta hurt that gal," he said to himself.

Tonight Tony tilted way back in his seat. Charles was sitting at the edge of his. Couldn't take his eyes off that sweet, scratchy voice and her smooth, luscious curves all dolled up in sheer royal blue.

Homeboy's gone, Tony laughed to himself. He smacked Charles across the back, got up and went to sit with a well-dressed man at the far end back table.

When Trudy finished the last set she slipped back inside the dressing room.

Trudy sat down and unzipped her blue gown. She was just about to peel it off when she heard rapid knocking at the door.

Bap, bap, bap.

"Who is it?" Trudy yelled out. Damn. Can't a girl get out her dress good before some hound comes sniffing for crumbs?

"Miss Trudy," the voice said through the thin wooden door. It was Sonny from the band.

"Miss Trudy, there's a man out there in the front row gimme ten dollars to hand you this paper. Said it was real important you got it." Sonny was hoping he could get in the room and have a look around. He hadn't been inside the dressing room before.

"I'm sorry, Sonny, but I'm not dressed just yet. Could you slide it under the door for me, please?" Trudy said through the crack.

She could hear the fumbling around outside, then saw the white flap of a crumpled sheet appear under the door. She didn't hear anything for a while and imagined Sonny still there on his hands and knees, breathing through the slim keyhole.

"Is that it, Sonny?" she said.

She heard a rumbling and a mild cough.

"Oh yeah, Miss Trudy, that's it. Thank you, ma'am. I'll tell the man you got it all right," Sonny said.

Trudy could hear his heavy feet sanding the hallway's floorboards.

Pearl laughed. "Girl, that boy loves your dirty drawers. He is so proud to be doing you a favor, he don't know what to say. I bet he'd hold your panties back to let yo' ass pee."

"Stop it, Pearl," Trudy said, laughing herself and unfolding the note.

"You know it's true. You ought to pay that boy some mind. Nothing wrong with getting a man who loves you more than you love him. Man who loves you more is sure to stay at home nights. Nothing wrong with him being a little on the ugly side neither. An ugly man would be so happy to have you. Wouldn't be pushing you over trying to get in your mirror like these pretty boys do. Ugly'll treat you right. Treat you like royalty. I've had two myself, so I know." Pearl smeared on more red lipstick.

But Trudy wasn't paying attention. She was reading the neat handwriting on the tiny note while sipping a glass of red wine.

"What's it say?" Pearl asked, trying to read over Trudy's shoulder.

"I'm not telling," Trudy said coyly. She crumpled the note and dropped it in the trash.

Shirley jerked open the door and hurried through the dressing room door. She'd been listening outside and saw the note on the floor and picked it up and read it out loud. "Dear lady in blue, please join me . . ."

"Don't be so nosy." Trudy snatched the note back and ripped it all up.

Shirley had a small cocktail apron over a black, clinging dress. She had already spotted the man in a well-tailored ivory-colored suit. She watched him scribbling a note and handing it to Sonny. She had come back in the dressing room to find out what it said. She had hated Trudy from the first day she'd come on. She felt she did most of the work around the club. Trudy didn't have to do nothing but stand on the stage and be cute. Besides, all the men wanted to talk to her now. She was squeezing out all Shirley's action.

Shirley peeked out a small hole drilled through the dressing room wall. You could see the whole club through the tiny peephole. Tony had it done so he could come down and look at who was in the club without them knowing he was there. She saw Sonny making his way back to the table with a man with dark shades and a diamond pinkie ring. The man thanked Sonny and placed a bill in his palm.

"You don't see many high-class niggas like him up in here," Shirley said, rapidly popping her gum.

"Let me see." Pearl looked out the peephole herself. She saw a handsome man in a beautiful woven suit. He sat in one of the red vinyl booths. He was smoking a thin Tiparillo, and his pinkies were all filled with diamonds. The man nodded now and then to people passing his table.

"Well, I'll be. He's all grown up, but that sho' 'nuff's him. All this damn time and he still ain't no good. Look how he's holding his spoon," Pearl said, disapproving.

Shirley looked at Pearl like she'd lost her damn mind. "Y'all act too suspicious sometime. Go on and keep yo' ugly-ass men if you want. I likes mine pretty and I likes mine rich. All I gotta do is swish my big ass. Nigga'd be paying my rent by the end of the week." Shirley popped her gum three times in Trudy's face and smiled.

Trudy looked at Shirley and smiled cruelly back. "That big ass of yours ain't been getting you much."

Pearl smirked and leaned farther toward the mirror, dousing her bosom with powder.

"You be acting too uppity lately." Shirley sneered at Trudy and then turned to Pearl. "Why you got to be so hard on the brother who got money? What'd he ever do to you?" Shirley asked Pearl.

"Oh, Cashflo be in here now and then, flashing them nice clothes and pretty-boy smile. Having his whispered conversations, big money changing hands, sending for champagne bottles and junk," Pearl said.

Trudy peeked out the hole to look too. Ah shit! she said to herself. That sure was him, sitting right there in front. The same one she'd seen in the black SUV. The one with the tan-suit man. What was he doing here?

Trudy dabbed her face and took a quick swig of water.

"What's wrong with you?" Shirley asked. "You look like you're sick."

"I hope you didn't snack on none of them wings before they got done." Pearl peeked out the small hole again. "Men like him make me sick too. The only thing a man like him cares about is money, and he ain't too concerned how he gets it. Your best bet is to stay put. Leave him alone. A man that high-class got to be dealing dirt. Oh, he'll take you whereever you want to go, as long as it's on his way."

"Maybe he got lucky and hit Lotto," Shirley added.

"Lotto, my ass. It's crack, if you ask me. He makes money sucking blood from the good folk in our community. I've seen many a mama sell her own flesh and bone just for one last hit.

Dope man has no soul but the dollar bill, girl. You don't *even* want to go there," Pearl said, disapproving.

"You don't even know him and now you got him selling dope. Black folks are the most suspicious folks on earth." Shirley placed her hand on her hip.

"Trudy'd be better off with somebody like Ray Ray," Pearl said, still dousing her large bosom.

Trudy kept her eyes down toward the floor. Everyone knew Ray Ray had just come from jail.

"I know he looks rough. But that's a real man, honey. Always respectful. Had yo' back from day one. He made a mistake but he paid for it, baby. I swear that young man done changed."

"Ray Ray?" Shirley laughed right in Pearl's face. "That black jailbird bum? That burned ragamuffin? Who in holy hell would want him? All that boy is a black walking scab."

"What the hell do you know about picking a good man? All you've had was something a gype dog drug in or what an old mangy cat wouldn't touch if it was drenched in nip. Now hush and just let me finish."

Shirley popped her gum loudly but sat down and remained quiet.

"We had this girl named Peaches, used to be at the club. Came by to help clean up and cook. She married this fella who drove them old tow trucks. Was always dragging some dead car around." Pearl laughed to herself and fanned at her bosom. "Black handsome man stood about six-foot-five, with some thick, wavy stuff he brushed down. Peaches would crack us up about that man's appetite." Pearl lowered her voice and looked around the room slyly. "And the girl wasn't talking about food." Pearl fanned herself again, smiling at the mirror. "Had two pretty babies. Two big fat, juicy boys. As cute as they wanted to be."

"Who cares," Shirley said, angrily sawing her nails. She was bored unless the conversation revolved around her. She'd heard enough of Pearl's backyard gossip.

"Now hold up, wait a minute. I'm fixin' to tell it." Pearl held up one of her hands. "Peaches showed up one day and Jimmy was there. That's his name, Jimmy. I recognized his slick gait a mile away. Pimp-walking, soul-stealing wannabe chump. His mother didn't want him down in San Diego no more. Dropped him down here every summer. He was five-and-dime then, a little street sucker who sold nickel bags and scratchers. So one day he starts flirting with Peaches at work. They were about the same age, and he'd wait for her on the sidewalk, talking while she swept outside. Next thing we know, she does a no-show the next morning. Nobody knew where she was. Her husband called up about ninety-eight times. Came on down here, holding a kid in each hand. Never did see her. Got turned out is what they say."

"You mean she never came back? You didn't see her again? You guys didn't file a police report or nothing?" Trudy asked.

"Yeah, she came back. Three and a half months later but I swear it wasn't the same girl. Face all broke out. Big gashes and scars. She used to have the smoothest complexion back then. Came back with her hair matted, wearing some worn, torn-up spandex, turned-over shoes and no socks. Yeah, she came back all right, long enough to get her poor husband's VCR and TV. Haven't seen hide nor hair of her since."

Trudy finished her makeup and looked back at Pearl.

"Well, what happened to that fine-ass husband of hers?" Shirley asked, interested now.

"Jail," Pearl said. She studied her lap. "I sure miss cooking for that overgrown boy. Man could sit up and eat hisself twenty-eight pancakes. But after what happened to Peaches, he was never the same. Losing poor Peaches shook the man to the bone. Poor thing was never the same. Spent most of his time in that truck hunting for Jimmy. But he'd never gotten a good look at Jimmy's face. He was going by build. Judging by type. Every fast-talking, game-runnin' punk made him sick. Lotta folks got whipped down that summer. But Jimmy didn't feel like duckin' and dodging no more. So he made a friend call saying he needed a tow, told the friend to use his name. Peaches's husband don't say nothing.

Pulls up to the curb slow. Shot that boy point-blank in the face."

"But that wasn't him! Didn't somebody tell? Obviously he shot the wrong man."

"Hell, yeah, they told, but so what? It's too late. And then Jimmy, who hadn't shown his punk ass in months, strolls into Dee's Parlor that very same day, sits there and orders a steak."

"Well, damn, Pearl," Shirley said, "it was clearly a mistake." Shirley licked her finger and held it to her thigh. She made a sizzling sound through her teeth with her tongue. "And when he gets out I got something for him." She smiled.

Pearl shook her finger in Shirley's dumb face. "That boy's serving hard time for murder, you fool. Your hot little ass gonna have to sit there and rot 'cause he ain't getting out again, honey."

Shirley spun in the stool like it was a ride. "Oh, like every man y'all had was a nice slice of pie. Pearl, you ain't exactly no Catholic school-teacher." Shirley smiled at the other two women. "Shoot, I seen a lotta y'alls men. Y'all pickin' off fleas just like everyone else."

Trudy stood up and got in Shirley's smirking face. "If I was as silly as you, I swear I'd bite my own tongue."

Pearl rolled her eyes. She patted her stomach. "Don't worry 'bout Shirley. She don't bother me none. Y'all know I didn't get this old being dumb."

Pearl turned back to Shirley and adjusted her

breasts. "Don't envy my mornings if you don't know my midnights. You ain't never once danced in my pumps. Hell, yeah, I had my share of ragamuffins and whatnot, but that's not what we're talking about here. I seen that shit buried down deep inside mean folks' eyes. Now maybe yours ain't used to spotting shit yet, but after working in nightclubs for over twenty-odd years, I'd say I was a better judge than yo' skinny tight ass. See, I watch eyes, baby. Eyes'll tell you everything you want to know. Teeth might be smiling, hands counting out money, but them eyes. Humph. Lord, chile, them eyes, they don't lie. Just as evil and mean as you please. See, the wave always goes back into the water and the devil's ready to sucker punch you again. I done already carried my own share of sorrow. Had two husbands I already done put in the ground. My first one, Lord, girl, we fought every night. Tearing up shit like wild cats and dogs. Rolling on the rug, him pulling my hair and me trying to scratch out his eyes. But I thought my sweet would rub off on him. Shoot, all I ended up with was rug burns. Girl, that man gave me hell, from Monday to Sunday, I'm talkin' H-E-L-L, hell! Man put the 'me' in mean 'cause that's all he was, mean to me. Finally gave me some peace when he keeled over and died."

"That has nothing to do with—" Shirley tried to interrupt again.

"Then I met Mr. Jefferson, my second husband." Pearl smiled up at the ceiling. "Sweet as potato pie. Happy all the time. Didn't have much money, you understand, but he always helped out. Kept our place spic and span, painting and planting those fruit trees we got. And I didn't find him at no church Easter Sunday."

No one knew where Pearl had met her last husband. There was a big patch of time missing out of his past. He'd done some time upstate but she'd never told anyone that. He was good now and that's all that mattered. And there were some things with Pearl you just didn't ask, and she didn't plan on telling them now. "See, some men's don't have much but a whole lot of heart. That's what I'm about. I don't tangle with mean, honey. Uh-uh, nosirree. Don't got nothing to do with cruel. You better keep them eyes peeled and watch your back, honey. Them slick ones might grin and they wallets be bulging, but their hearts, girl, are blacker than tar."

Trudy looked out the peephole again. Two big, burly men sat, flanking each side of Jimmy. She'd have to be careful. Watch each step she made. Pearl might act real country sometimes, but she wasn't one to be lying. But with fear easing in, Trudy was still determined. She wouldn't change her plan out of fear of one man. She'd handle him, was all. Like she handled the others. Flirt a bit but stay noncommittal. There was no way she'd turn into somebody's dumb junkie. All she wanted was money. A chance to get out. She wasn't taking much. She wouldn't be greedy. Trudy studied the man's coal-black eyes a long time.

He was a hurdle. No bones about that. But he'd definitely be her last.

# 17

## Trudy and Jimmy

When Trudy finished her set she pulled through the bar. It was like trying to get off an overstuffed bus.

"Let me buy you a drink, precious."

"Can I ask you a quick question?"

"Come'ere, gal, and sit on Big Papa's lap."

Trudy mildly smiled as she wiggled through tables. Finally she found Vernita's table. Vernita was sitting between two older men. She'd been in the bar for less than ten minutes and had them both eating out of her hand. One bought her a drink and the other hooked his arm around her chair while she stroked the fine hair on the back of his neck.

"I told you, go bald," Vernita whispered inside Trudy's ear. Vernita's hair was less than a quarter-inch long. "Girl, you pull in a whole different man."

"Watch," Vernita said, standing up. "I'ma fool around and dance with 'em both." Vernita got up, and both men stood too. They looked like they'd follow her right into the ocean. "He-ey," Vernita said and batted her eyes. "If I gotta go play a white girl on Friday, I might as well be ghetto tonight!"

Trudy laughed watching Vernita dance on the floor sandwiched between two happy men. She'd never seen nothing so raunchy.

Vernita was one who could ignite any party. She was a flare on a dull, dusty road.

All Trudy needed now was to square things with Charles. Her eyes skimmed around the dark edges of the room.

A tall man in black sunglasses approached her chair.

"Excuse me, miss. My friend over there wants to know if you'll join him." Trudy glanced over at Jimmy. He smiled and lifted his glass. Tony was sitting beside him.

"Well, why can't your friend come and ask me himself?"

The man seemed annoyed at Trudy's response and walked quickly back toward his table. He whispered in Jimmy's ear. Jimmy looked up and nodded. He stood up, gliding toward where

Trudy sat, shaking hands and giving pounds along the way.

"Look at that," Pearl whispered to Shirley. "What'd I say? Everybody knows the dope man's name."

"So what?" Shirley sneered. "All I see is money."

"Hello," Jimmy said to Trudy. "May I join you for a moment?" His two boys sat at a table nearby and he moved his chair close to her shoulder.

Pearl walked by and looked down at him hard.

"Evening," Jimmy said.

Pearl just ignored him and disappeared backstage.

Jimmy waved for Shirley to bring a bottle of champagne.

Shirley sat the bottle down a little too rough. She scratched her giant hair and left.

A burly man sat down at the table a moment. He whispered something to Jimmy and then got up and left too.

"Looks like you lost your friend," Trudy said, looking back at the man.

"Looks like I found me a new one." His smile showed a row of dazzling-white, straight teeth.

His shoulders looked like you could build homes on them. There was something else she saw too, something deep inside his eyes. It was as if he looked right through her, right into her bones. Trudy quickly looked away.

"I'm sorry," Trudy said, standing up, "I was on my way to see my friend." Trudy looked around for Vernita.

"Just sit for a minute and talk to me. Please." Jimmy was mildly holding her arm.

Trudy had never met any rich men in Dee's Parlor before. Oh, there were plenty of those who acted like they had cash. Tommy and Edmond, Darren and Shaun. They all dressed expensive. Went to restaurants and stuff. But none of them knew a job if it knocked 'em upside the head, and half of 'em still lived off their mamas. Nobody had real money. Not no deep-pocket cash, and they sure never gave any to her.

It was so loud in Dee's Parlor that Jimmy put his lips to Trudy's ear to speak. She could feel his warm breath on her neck. She was praying Charles didn't walk in and see her like this. Trudy nervously watched the front door.

"So you're Trudy," Jimmy said, smiling, leaning back in his seat and opening his legs wide. "I thought you were a church girl singing like that up there. I'da sworn up and down it was Sunday."

Trudy licked the cherry she picked from her

glass. She noticed his purple silk tiepin, covered with diamonds and a giant diamond and sapphire ring.

"My name is James, but everybody calls me Jimmy. I got your name from the drummer over there. Had to give him ten dollars for the privilege. But," he said, gently squeezing her wrist, "I'd say it was money well spent."

"So tell me," Trudy asked, stroking the length of his tie, "how do you make yours?" She was never afraid to ask a straight question. It kept people on the defensive.

"Oh, so you one of them types likes to know everything?" Jimmy said.

"I just like to know who I'm dealing with, is all."

"Oh, we dealing already?" he said, opening his eyes wide and smiling. "Then I guess it's okay if we dance."

Before Trudy could protest, he stood up and pulled her hand.

"Shit," he said under his breath as he watched Trudy's hips weave through the tables toward the dance floor.

Trudy felt his gaze, but hell, what could she could do? Besides, there was something about him she liked. There was sureness about him, a confidence too. Like he was used to silver spoons and linen napkins. That casualness rich people had.

So when Trudy felt his honey-brown eyes ease

into her backside, she dipped her hips some, winding them real nice and slow, giving him something to make his mouth water.

Oh, God, she thought, don't let Charles come in and see me now.

He circled Trudy's waist and she placed her arms around his neck. She could feel the heavy fabric of his jacket under her hands. Hmmm, she said to herself. This was cashmere. From all the clothes Trudy stole, she'd learned a few things about fabrics.

"So are you going to tell me, or do I have to beg?" As much as this man felt good next to her stomach, Trudy wanted to see if he'd say what he did. She knew he dealt dirt. She knew asking was dangerous but she wanted to watch Jimmy squirm.

Jimmy gripped her firm waist a little more snugly. "You seem like a woman who knows what she wants." He ever so gently tugged a handful of her braids until she had to stare up at his face. "But just tell me this"—his lips grazed her throat—"how bad do you want to know?"

Trudy pulled her braids out of his hand. "Don't you think what you do says a lot about who you are?" She was playing with fire, but damn this was fun.

"No," Jimmy said flatly. "Uh-uh, not really. Not unless you're the type that judges people by their jobs. The kind of person who puts a price tag on somebody's back." There wasn't nothing

Jimmy liked better than messing with people's minds. He loved to throw nosy folks off his track.

"Listen, baby, I found you in a club, right? You sing, okay. But I'm pretty sure you're a helluva lot more than that."

Trudy smiled. *Yeah, fool. I work at the bank.* She wasn't about to say that.

"Oh, it's okay. I know you want to play twenty questions so you can try to define me. Try and pigeonhole my ass. Listen, I'll make it easy for you, okay? I'll just come right out and say it. I'm in the commodities business, baby," Jimmy said directly. "Stocks and bonds. Transactions and shit. You know, buy low, Dow Jones, all that drama." Jimmy stopped dancing and straightened his tie. "Satisfied?"

"You play the stock market game?" Trudy asked as he pulled her to him again.

"Yeah, and that's just what it is, a muthafuckin' game." He was grinding against her, pulling her closer to his chest. Trudy could feel the raw heat radiating from his skin. Just then a burly man came behind Jimmy and tapped him on the shoulder. He leaned over and whispered something in his ear.

"Listen, baby," Jimmy said to Trudy, "I have to handle some business. Is it okay if I call you later?" He still had both arms wrapped around her waist.

Trudy usually didn't like men who called her "baby" right away. Pearl said men used "baby" so they didn't have to remember names. All Trudy knew was her mother called her man Mr. Hall and that sounded like he was her boss.

But Jimmy said it so low and it sounded so sexy, Trudy didn't mind at all. Trudy didn't make a habit of giving out her number either. In fact, she had a rule against it. She dated this one fool named Roger who started to stalk her. After that she had to be careful. But there was something about this man. His wide, cocky smile, the way his eyes speared her body. His elegant, well-groomed demeanor. But there was something extra, too. That little touch of ghetto. That faint taste of street. That hard, manly edge that she loved. Vernita used to call it an addiction.

"Your thug-life men gonna get your ass twisted," Vernita said all the time.

She remembered how hard it was to get rid of Roger. She had to get call blocking on that freak.

Trudy was smiling, with Jimmy's hands trying to creep to her ass, when she suddenly saw Charles walk in.

"Follow me," Trudy said, leading Jimmy down the hall. She didn't want Charles to see her talking to Jimmy at all. She smiled at Jimmy and then opened her purse, taking out a matchbook and pen.

"Here," he said, turning all the way around. "You can write on my back."

Trudy placed the small cardboard against his

broad shoulders. She could feel Jimmy's thick muscles underneath his cream coat. She wanted to caress his huge, bulging neck but instead slowly scribbled her number. She knew it was dangerous having this man get this close. She knew she was playing with a whole box of matches. But there was something about him Trudy couldn't resist. Maybe she could have some hot, quick fun for a minute. He could be her last taste before she left town. Like a mint you sucked right before steak.

# 18

## Trudy and Charles

Trudy waved to Charles to come near the cigarette machine.

She hoped Charles hadn't seen her talking to Jimmy. See, Charles was the main hinge in Trudy's bank-robbing scheme. Charles was the mail carrier on the Dee's Parlor block. She would watch his gray pants and large leather satchel. Charles was perfect. His occupation played an integral part in her plan. She couldn't do the job without him.

"Come on," she told him. "Let's talk outside."

"It's kinda dark outside," Charles said, following her feet.

"That's okay," Trudy said, walking ahead, her stilettos tapping the concrete.

Trudy jumped into her gray Honda and twisted the key. The car revved but it wouldn't turn over. Trudy tried it again. She gave it more gas but this time it didn't even catch. There was enough juice in the engine for the car to rev once but now it only clicked and went dead.

"You probably flooded it now," Charles said, peering in her window.

Trudy frowned. She pretended to be upset. "Really?" she said, making her voice disappointed, but inside she was just as pleased as pie.

"You have to wait a few minutes before you can start it."

Trudy banged the steering wheel hard for effect.

"Pop the hood," Charles said. He looked inside the engine, but he didn't have a clue about cars.

Trudy sat nervously in the front seat. She hoped he wouldn't see she'd unhooked the cables.

"Might be your alternator." Charles shut the hood. He was anxious to talk to Trudy about Flo. He wanted to know what she knew. Then, suddenly, two loud voices came bursting from the club. Their laughter filled the whole lot.

It was Percy and Ray Ray. Trudy pulled the lever on her seat until she was almost lying flat in the car.

"Maybe it's better if we talk away from here," Trudy said.

"Yeah," he agreed. "I can give you a ride if you

want." Charles could hardly believe his good luck. In a second she'd be in his car!

Trudy looked at him like she was uneasy. Then she grabbed her purse from the backseat and got out.

"That's okay, my friend can come get me," she said. Trudy walked over to the pay phone and pretended to call Vernita. She knew Vernita had left the club to see Lil Steve. "No use wasting all this good liquor," she'd said when she left.

A vicious smile had slithered across her lips, as Trudy watched Vernita leave. Vernita was going to meet Lil Steve and give him the when, where and why. Everything was working out fine.

Trudy slammed the receiver and walked back to Charles.

"You sure it's no problem?" Trudy asked, fingering her long braids. She covered one breast with a handful of hair. The other breast loomed huge in the moon.

Charles held the door and Trudy wiggled into his Buick. He watched the seat belt dive into her chest. As soon as he turned on the car he started asking questions.

"So what do you know," Charles asked her point-blank.

Trudy pulled Charles's hand to her lap. "Look, I'm not trying to get in your business, but I saw something last Friday at the bank. Something I think you should know."

"What?" Charles said, smiling. What could this cutie-pie have seen? His hand tucked in hers, Charles wanted to touch the rest of her body.

Trudy gently brought his palm to her lips. "I work at the B of A on Wilshire, okay?"

"So," Charles said, smiling. "What's that supposed to mean?" Charles had no idea what Trudy was going to say, so he still continued to joke. "What, you want me to open another account?"

Trudy held his hand close. "When Flo came into the bank, she got in my line."

Charles wrinkled his face. He pulled back his hand. "So what are you trying to say?"

"Look, don't be mad, I just thought you should know. Flo came in and withdrew eight thousand dollars."

Charles bit the inside meat of his hand. "Wait a minute. What are you talking about?"

"Flo came to my line. I gave her the money."

"All of it? Most of that money was mine!" Charles banged his hand real hard against the dash.

"All but the five bucks the bank makes you leave to keep the account open," Trudy said.

"Fuck!" Charles yelled, banging his hand again. "I'ma get her, I swear!"

"No!" Trudy said. "Don't be dumb, Charles. All you'll end up doing is going to jail or at the emergency unit at King Drew."

Charles scowled hard. He was too mad to talk.

"Look, I know you owe Tony."

"Day-am!" Charles said. "You know all of my business!"

"Tony has a big mouth." Trudy pulled back his palm. She placed his hand over her breast. "Look, I know you have a good heart. I see you work hard. And I can help if you let me."

Charles was a hurricane of emotions. He'd never been so pissed off in all his life, but he was touching Trudy's amazing body and couldn't stop squeezing her fresh-melon breasts.

"Dammmmn," Charles said again, but it was more like a moan, and the car windows steamed from his breath.

"I can help you," Trudy said, tracing her thumb along his thigh.

"Yeah?" Charles said, trying to get on top of her. "What can you do for me, huh?"

"Why don't you start by turning on your engine and taking me home," Trudy said.

Charles started the car and she rolled down the window. She watched the small stars in the sky.

"I have a plan," Trudy said.

"Really?" he said, squeezing her thigh. He couldn't wait to get her home. He drove down Venice like a fiend. "I hope your plan includes me."

"It's about getting some money, that's all I can say."

"Is it dangerous?" Charles had an aversion to crime. Too many of his old friends were now doing time.

"No. Not the part you have to play. Drop me off here—that's where I stay." They were already at Western. Trudy unlocked the door. "I'll call you and tell you more tomorrow."

"Why can't you tell me all about it right now?" Charles pulled over. He wrapped his arms around her waist.

Trudy let him squeeze her before opening her car door.

"Can I walk you up?" Charles asked, hopeful. He was upset with himself for letting an opportunity pass. He tried to grab her arm and clung to her blouse. He heard the faint sound of a tear.

"Hey, wait a second. Let go," Trudy scolded him now. "Tomorrow we'll have plenty of time."

Trudy turned around and flashed him a generous grin. She cupped his chin in her hand. "Give me your number and I'll call you tomorrow."

Ripping an envelope in half, he scribbled his number, handing her the torn paper. He knew giving Trudy his home number was risky but after what Charles had heard tonight, he just didn't care anymore.

Trudy waved and waited until Charles took off. Then she walked the short block to the end of the street and went into her real apartment across the street. She didn't want anyone to know where she lived. She quickly went in and bolted her door. She didn't want Charles. She knew he was Flo's. All she wanted to do was tease him. Float him along. Get his mind right so he'd help her with her plan.

Poor Charles. Some men where such dumb Chihuahuas. Half of 'em would do backflips if you'd just let 'em smell it. Lord knows that boy's nose was blown open wide. He was desperate for cash and had weak, roaming eyes. He was going to work out just fine.

But Charles had certain ideas of his own. He smelled Trudy's cologne on the back of his hand and drove home with a brand-new ambition.

# 19

## *Flo and Charles*

When Charles left home that night, Flo paced the living room floor. She kept looking out the window and walking back and forth.

"I know Charles is up to something," she said out loud to herself.

She watched TV for a while and then clicked it off, tossing the remote across the floor.

"Dammit, I feel it. I know something's up. That asshole's backsliding again." She walked to the kitchen and popped open a Coke.

"If I could just catch him," she said to herself. Flo finished the Coke and squeezed the can with her hands. She fingered the new car key with her thumb. Having the car made Flo realize she wanted something more.

"If I could just catch him in the act." Flo grabbed a sweater and the rest of her keys. She was determined to go see what was happening at Dee's. The screen door slammed loud when she left.

In the heart-attack section of L.A. they stayed in, there was only one club worth putting your foot in. That was Dee's Parlor off Washington and Tenth.

Flo ran down the street, jumped in the car and drove down to Dee's like a dope fiend. She clicked off her lights when she got close. She didn't want anyone to see her pull up. And she sure didn't want Charles to know she had sunk so low as to trail his fucking punk ass. She'd seen those dumb women showing up at clubs. All of them looking beat-down, torn-up and sad, screaming "Leroy! Tyrone! I know you in here." Flo'd never give Charles that satisfaction.

Flo kept her lights low until she could see the pale neon floating in the dark, murky sky. There happened to be a little side street sitting directly across from Dee's Parlor. It was the perfect spot to watch who went in and out. That's where Flo parked. Her car was only three away from the front, but the street was so tree-lined and the night was so black, no one could see she was there. Flo spotted Charles's raggedy car in the lot. Percy and Ray Ray were talking outside. She definitely didn't want any of those who-rahs to see her. They looked too gangsterish for her.

It was starting to get cold. Flo wrapped a sweater around her shoulders. No matter how hot L.A. got by day, it could get downright freezing at night. She scooted down in the seat and kept her eyes on Dee's door and her rearview mirrors. This was not a very nice street. She didn't need any surprises.

Flo watched the steady flow of folks coming out the door. Working stiffs in uniforms, a few suits and ties and some stumbling drunks glued to hoochies wearing Band-Aids as skirts and big, lumpy, stiff push-up bras. They laughed or talked serious and lit their smokes while panhandlers hounded them for dimes.

Flo sat parked on the dark side of pain for two hours. After a while she started rolling her hair. She had to be at work early in the morning, so she'd brought her rollers in a plastic grocery bag. Besides, stupid Charles would never suspect she'd been out if her hair was all rolled up already.

Finally she recognized Charles's build at the door. She eased farther up in the seat to make sure. Yeah, that was Charles, all right. He was waiting by the pay phone next to this big-ass chick in a skimpy, low-cut top. The girl turned around and Flo looked right into Trudy's face.

"Well, ain't this a bitch!" Flo said under her breath and sat even farther up in her seat so she could see. She watched Charles help Trudy get in his car. "So she's the one got Charles's nose open wide." She watched Charles and Trudy drive off.

*I knew it! I knew he was stepping out again.*

"That bitch ain't got no shame at all," Flo said out loud. She watched Charles's taillights fade to black.

"Well, hell, I guess it's every damn woman for herself." Flo didn't even bother to buckle up when she pulled off. Her tires skidded away from the curb.

"If her mama helped herself to a damn married man, that shit must just run in the family."

As Flo followed them, her heart began to beat fast. She was so mad she could barely sit there and think.

Charles took Adams all the way down to Western.

Probably going to the Mustang Hotel, Flo said to herself. She knew about the Mustang from going with Tony. There were lots of hourly rate motels in L.A. Lots of them lined LaBrea Avenue near the Number 10 Freeway. But nothing compared to Mustang. The Mustang was huge. It was a three-story structure that took up the whole block with giant mirrors glued to the ceiling and walls. Flo was so distracted with these thoughts, she almost hit the car stopped in front of her at the light. She was panting so loud the sound filled her ears. Flo lingered back when she saw Charles's car stop.

"Oh," Flo said, "they must be going to her place."

Flo looked at the apartment across the street. It was nasty and its lawn was filled with trash.

Flo watched Trudy wave to Charles by the curb and then dash across the lawn and to an apartment farther down the street. That place was fifty times worse than the first.

Flo had to run a few lights to beat Charles home. She parked her new car down the street under some trees. She threw on her robe and kicked off her shoes. She turned on the TV and opened another bag of chips just before Charles pushed through the door.

"Oh, so Mr. Backslider decided to come home." Flo didn't say that, but that's what she thought. She sucked her teeth while pulling her robe over her gut. Her foot was flung over the set so she could get better reception. Charles noticed the hair on her knees.

Charles walked past her. He stopped in the kitchen. He opened the fridge to get a cold beer, drinking the whole thing while leaning his face on the ice tray.

In the freezing cold, Charles's whole body still blazed. He couldn't believe Flo had taken their money. He stayed in the kitchen, waiting in the dark, drinking some Johnnie Walker straight from the bottle.

Flo couldn't take the cold silence anymore. "You paying the light bill this month," she yelled to Charles.

"You the one got every damn light on in here. Got radios going in rooms you're not even in." Charles walked through the apartment, flicking switches and yanking the cords from the wall until all that was left was the cool, icy blue of the TV. Charles yanked the set right from the wall. "You got a lot of nerve talking to me about bills."

Flo knew Charles might know something. But she wasn't sure what. All she knew was that she had just seen Charles with Trudy and she was steaming inside just like him.

He snatched off his shoes and yanked down his pants and tore into the bed with his boxers.

Flo never said another word. She was too plain disgusted. She brushed her teeth and fell into bed. She couldn't shake this flu and was getting more and more tired. She didn't have the strength to fight—besides, what could she say? All she saw was Charles giving Trudy a ride. But her anger still burned. She was frustrated and upset. What was he doing with Trudy? Why did he need to give her a ride? Flo lay under the covers but just couldn't take it. She tore off the sheet and sat up in bed. Finally, she had to speak up.

"I saw you," Flo said, clicking on the bedroom lamp.

Charles said nothing. He rolled to his side. He breathed in and let the air out slowly. He did not want to kill anyone tonight.

"I saw you. I saw her get into your car."

But Charles said nothing. He breathed deeply under the sheet. He was straining not to rip it in half.

Flo stared at his covered-up, muscular body.

Flo shook him. "Hey, I'm talking to you, boy. I know you hear me, Charles. Stop trying to pretend you're asleep."

Charles sat up, yanking the sheet to his waist. "You got a lot of fucking nerve," Charles told Flo, rolling the tight sheet over his head.

But Flo grabbed the sheet and yanked it back down. "I saw you with Trudy. I know it was her."

"Oh, you're spying on me now? Ain't this a trip. You steal all my money and now you're spying on me too. Don't say shit to me, you damn thief!"

Charles boldly sat up. He stared at her hard. He wanted to see what Flo had to say.

Flo looked down. She fixed one of her loose rollers. "Answer me first," she said quietly, looking down.

"What? What the hell do you want to know? I saw the girl. Her car broke. I took the chick home. Shit, I'm here with yo' ass. Get the fuck off my back."

Flo's scowling face looked plain without makeup. Her globe head was lumpy with curlers. She really felt bad; she felt nauseous and sick.

"Now answer me something!" Charles yelled in her face. "What the fuck did you do with my cash?"

Damn! He found out. She was in dangerous water. She didn't know what else to say, so she clicked off the light, but Charles clicked it right back on.

"Hey, I'm talking to you, huh!" Charles violently shook her. "God damn it, Flo, that was our down-payment money. What the hell did you do with it, huh?"

"So the bitch fuckin' told you. I knew that she would." Flo was so sick with anger, she almost threw up.

"Where's the money, Flo, huh? What'd you do with my cash?" Charles started tearing up the room, pulling out drawers. He knocked over a lamp and it crashed to the floor. "What did you do with it, huh?"

"Your money?" Flo screamed. "Some of that was mine!"

"Where's the money, Flo, huh?" Charles knocked over a cabinet. It crashed like a 6.9 earthquake.

Flo couldn't stand watching the room turn into a disaster.

"I spent it!" Flo yelled.

"What? Spent it on what?"

"You wouldn't have done anything but gamble it away!"

"What did you spend all my money on, huh?" Charles's face was twisted with rage.

"You would have spent it too!" she said defensively. "Besides, some of it was mine!"

"You know most of that cash came straight from my check!" Charles grabbed her shoulders. He started shaking Flo hard.

It was late. The man upstairs banged his broom against the floor. "Would you country fools shut the fuck up!"

"What did you spend it on, huh?"

"A car!" Flo yelled back, trying to square up her shoulders. "I went out and bought a new car!" Flo said it loud, like she was proud of the fact, but inside, her body felt like a rag.

Charles wanted to bash his fist into her face. Instead he slammed his fist into the wall over the bed. The plaster broke all the way down to the wood, and huge chunks fell over their pillows.

"Well, where is it, huh? If you're so righteous, then why are you hiding it, huh?"

Flo stared at the ceiling and said low, "It's not hidden. It's parked in front."

"No, it isn't. I didn't see shit when I pulled in. You knew you were wrong. You knew this was foul. Because if you were right you would have parked the thing right in the driveway!"

Flo stared down at the floor.

Charles wondered what he'd ever seen in Flo in the first place.

Then he remembered. It was her hair. Thick, black, gorgeous hair that was so bold and bouncy. Bobbing like it had a mind of its own. Just like Flo. It was that wild hair he noticed first when she'd stepped off the bus that one morning. He couldn't even see her face, just that springy mop covering her eyes as she threw her purse over her shoulder.

When she finally did look his way she had the wildest flashing smile set in the smoothest black skin he'd ever seen. Charles had pretended to be examining some letters, waiting for her to get closer.

"Good morning," she'd told him as she walked down the street.

"Good morning," he'd said back, watching her open her gate.

"Girl, you got a million-dollar smile," he'd told her.

Charles remembered when Flo curled her hair to see him. Big shiny black curls with the sweet smell of Murray's or the slight hint of coconut oil.

Charles loved it when Flo got her hair done. Smiling all pretty, looking sexy and proud. Back then, it was all for him.

That was a long time ago, Charles thought to himself. And although she'd stuck with him after he'd had the affair, after he'd called her and begged her to please take him back, looking at her now in this awful, messed-up room, he could not for the life of him think of why he wanted her now. She had gotten a lot fatter since he'd moved in with her too, with them pies and cakes she made all the time. But he never imagined she'd take their money. He never thought she'd go that low.

Charles looked over at Flo's thickening waist. And that hair. Always rolled up. Always pulled tight. He rarely saw it out of them curlers no more. Charles glanced at Flo's hairnetted skull. She looked like an astronaut from hell. Only time he thought it really looked nice was when she stepped out the door to go to work.

Saving it for them white boys at her job, Charles thought. Never lets me touch it. Even making love she fussed about it all the time.

"Don't touch it so rough."

"Don't mess with my rollers."

"Hurry up, or you'll sweat out my 'do."

Every morning when he woke, Flo was lying next to him in those old dried-up curlers. By the time he got home, she had already changed from her pretty work clothes and her whole head was rolled, wearing some old, sloppy sweats.

Charles smashed an old empty beer can against the headboard and tossed it right on the floor. Flo got up and went into the bathroom. He could hear her softly crying. That made Charles sick to no end. He tore off his boxers, stretching naked over the mattress, staring at the hairbrush on the nightstand. The dense smell of hair drenched in coconut oil completely filled the whole room.

Flo stayed in the bathroom for a real long

time. When she came out she quickly slipped into bed.

Charles never looked Flo's way. He couldn't believe she'd spent their money. Taking that money killed his dream of having a house. It eliminated his cushion, the breathing room he thought he had. Having that money gave him some slack. He held it in but almost cried. What about Tony? What if he demanded his cash? His teeth gnawed the inside wall of his hand. What really ate him up was that Flo had gotten it first. This burned his skin to no end. Charles swiped the hairbrush down to the floor. He lay in the dark, watching Flo's heavy stomach slowly rise up and fall down.

Flo wore an orange lacy teddy; the panties had no crotch, and her large breasts tugged at the fabric. She hoped Charles's seeing the teddy would distract him a bit. She had held out, but now she really wanted to make up. If they made love, maybe they might be able to work something out. So even though the straps cut her arm and the seams felt too tight, Flo laid quiet, taking small mini breaths, dangling one leg daringly over the edge, hoping Charles would roll over and notice.

But Flo didn't know the depth of Charles's rage. She didn't realize how deep in debt Charles was and how much trouble that debt put him in.

Charles lay in bed blazing. He bit his whole

fist. He felt like he was boxed in a narrowing cage. He decided to give her a taste of her own medicine. He wanted her to crave it, make her starve for his body and then lie there and not give her nothing. The same way she had done him. He saw her through the small space along the bathroom door. He saw her lotion her body and douse it with fragrance and put a silk scarf over her hair. But Charles never budged; he ignored her completely and kept his eyes glued to the cracked, peeling ceiling, and eventually he drifted off to sleep.

Flo watched Charles sleep near the edge of the bed. She'd never seen Charles this angry before. She rolled all the way to her side and slept in a tight little ball.

In the morning, Charles looked at Flo with disgust. There was only one thing stuck in Charles's mind. Trudy's breasts, the arch of Trudy's dark nipples. Charles's body began to thicken, and his muscles grew taut. The warm fluid between his legs began to stiffen. Finally he just couldn't take any more. He seized Flo and rolled on top of her body. He parted her legs with one knee between her thighs. He drove into her body again and again, until her frame hung way off the bed.

"You want some of this, don'tcha?" Charles plunged more deeply. Her rollers wildly shook to and fro. As he rammed the bed, some of Flo's curlers fell to the floor.

"You like it, don't you?" Charles said, squeezing her breasts. Flo wanted to yelp but she bit her own tongue. She didn't want to complain; she didn't want to stop him. All she felt was guilt over taking their money. If she gave him some maybe he'd stop being so awful.

But Charles was crazy. His lust was inflamed. Finally Flo had to complain.

"Slow it down, baby. Don't be so rough."

But Charles wouldn't go slow. He got even rougher. His hot body surged, he was full throttle now. With each wild stroke he was paying Flo back. A heart-attack madness ran through his veins. He was dizzy with rage and boiling on top. He was struggling against the desire to grab at her throat and choke the life out of her frame. The money, he thought. All his money was gone. He wanted to strike her, to gouge out her eyes. The thought of having no money made him want to break down. But the anger dried the wet from his eyes.

There was a deep pleasure he got from being so completely vile. Like a drunk beating his kid when he got smashed. And just when he thought he couldn't take any more, just when he believed he could kill with his fury, he came with a force that knocked the wind from his lungs. He came with an evilness he'd never felt before. And like a broken racehorse before that final shot, Charles slumped to a stony, dead heap across Flo's chest.

There were only two things on his lunatic mind. Two crystal thoughts that stayed lodged in his body. All he wanted to do was get Trudy like this and get his hands on a whole bunch of money.

# 20

## Trudy and Tony

Trudy was about to sneak out when the handle turned and Tony pushed his way in.

"Lord have mercy! It's hotter than a whore's pussy after midnight out there. I swear I barely got out of Miss Williams's place alive. Good God almighty!" Tony dabbed his bald head. "Woman had on one of them long see-through numbers . . . whatchu call them things? Negga what's—negga leys thangs. What's that shit called, again?"

"Negligee," Trudy said without looking up.

Along with singing, Tony hired her to do light work in the bar's office. He liked having something pretty around while he worked. Besides the club, Tony had a side business lending money.

"Yeah, one of them nice neg-la-shays. Mercy. All that black meat, all spicy and hot. Woman

had no drawers to save her natural-born life."
Tony dabbed a handkerchief around his damp
brow. "I know it was there, just as sweet-smelling
and ready." He dabbed his head again and took
a big gulp of water, smashing the white paper
cup in his hand. "I couldn't see it, but I know'd
it was there. I could barely hold the paper for
her to sign." Tony's large body sat heavily on the
couch. "I swear I'm getting too old for this job."

Tony stared at Trudy and lowered his voice.
"The owner of the liquor store across the street
has been sobbing all morning. Seems like somebody broke in his building last night. Stole that
poor man's place blind."

Tony looked at Trudy. His eyes locked on her
face.

Why the hell was Tony looking at her like that,
Trudy thought. She didn't have a thing to do
with that liquor store robbery. But Trudy still
felt guilty. She avoided Tony's eyes. She felt the
creeping dead weight of those heavy-lidded
eyes. Guilt lived inside Trudy's veins every day.
Guilt loomed even when she hadn't done the
crime. She still felt responsible. She felt like
everyone knew it was her. It was one of the symp-
toms of stealing so long. You lived life feeling
just like a suspect.

Suddenly a police officer pushed into Tony's
small office.

"Ma'am?" the officer said. "I need to ask you
some questions."

Trudy was worried. Why did they want to talk to her?

"Were you here yesterday morning?" the police officer asked.

"Yeah, she was here," Tony chimed in.

The officer glared at Tony and looked back at her. "Did you see anything? Any suspicious-looking people?"

Trudy was trying not to look suspicious herself. "No," she said, looking in the officer's eyes.

He was a white, blond-haired man in a tight uniform. The black shirt and pants were so snug around his body, the uniform looked painted on his skin. In L.A., the cops don't play. You can wave, say hello, but you won't get no answer. They all have the flat, expressionless face of a statue.

"I didn't see a thing." Trudy told the officer. "I only work here part time."

The officer scribbled something down without looking at Trudy. He took out a business card from his breast pocket and, using his pointer finger, he pushed it across Trudy's desk. "Call me," he said, "if you remember anything at all." He stared at her awhile before clicking in his pen.

The officer's sunglasses slipped and she could see his blue eyes.

Trudy breathed deeply and took a sip of water. She fanned herself with some papers when the cop left.

"What's wrong with you, huh? You know something about that robbery?" Tony opened his sagging briefcase, took out a handful of papers, picked up the phone and started dialing. Trudy stayed at her desk and pretended to be busy, keeping her back toward Tony's face.

"Any calls? How's your mama? Everybody all right? Lord, Mr. Hall don't know what he got, um! If I had a mind—Hello, Miss Wesley. Yes, I was there this morning. . . . What did Sharon say 'bout the house?"

Tony went into his routine of mindless chitchat, but it always ended with the same exact line: "So when can I pick up my money?"

Tony let a few locals drink a little bit on credit but he always came by to get paid.

Trudy listened to him talking to one of his old drinking friends.

"I tol' you not to marry that woman, Eugene. You'd only seen her in the club lighting, man. Don't never marry no woman you ain't seen in the sun. I tol' you that woman was old."

"Trudy," he hollered out, "I'm leaving now. I got to get over to Miss Jenkins's place today. Tell yo' mama I said hello."

"Tell her yourself," Trudy said, not looking up.

Tony walked back into the office and leaned against her desk. He was struggling to get his short, beefy arm into his way-too-small jacket.

"Girl, why you got to be so ugly this morning?

Your mama's good people. Got a nasty tongue sometimes, but that's 'cause she got a huge chip on her shoulder."

"Why? What did the world do to her?" Trudy slammed a file drawer hard with her hip.

"It's Hall. He's been selling her wolf tickets for years. Promising her he'd leave his wife and he ain't never gonna do shit. Poor woman wasted her life on that fool."

"Poor woman! Tony, please," Trudy said. "Don't go sugarcoating it for me."

Tony looked at Trudy like she was a kid. The kind with hot-fire emotion but didn't know jack.

"Now, listen here, girl. I was there too. Everyone thinks your mama stole Mr. Hall. But your mama was Mr. Hall's woman first. Way back when Hall only worked as a clerk. Hall hovered over your mother when your daddy passed that year. Brought her candy and magazines and big jugs of ice cream and all the scotch whiskey she could drink. You weren't but two when y'all lived over in Watts. Stayed in a tiny unit over his store, and even though your apartment was small, it was stuffed full of everything he stocked."

Trudy bit a hangnail off her thumb. She knew this already. She sat quiet and bored. Tony wasn't saying nothing new.

"But Hall's business started to boom. He opened up another liquor store over off Vernon and that big one he got over off King. Your mother's sharp mind helped Hall buy them stores. But lots of things change when folks start tasting money. As Hall became rich, he saw your mama less and less and for three weeks he didn't come over at all."

"How do you know that?" Trudy asked him point-blank.

"Back then, me and Hall was good friends." Tony laughed.

"Man, that was one crazy cat. Glory me! We used to play Spades in the yard every Monday. That nigga talked more shit!" Tony dabbed his forehead with his hanky. A cloud passed over his face. "But money changed Hall. He didn't have time for his friends. Naw, Hall's eyes only had dollar signs in 'em. That's when he started on this church girl cross-town. Joan pitched a fit when she found out about that gal. She wasn't very pretty. Not no looker like your mother and was definitely not as good in the sack, 'cause he told me."

Trudy pushed the rusted-out file cabinet hard. This talk about her mother made her sick.

"But that church girl had something that Hall really wanted. Her daddy owned that big, giant furniture store, and that girl was his last living kin. All hell broke loose that hot summer, girl. You remember the Rodney King beating and them riots in '92? Well, a year before that, a Korean woman blasted a girl in her store. Shot that black chile in the back over a bottle of juice. When that gung-ho bitch only got probation for the crime, a lot of places got fire-bombed and burned. That church girl's father got killed defending his store. Hall married the girl and never did tell your mother. Six months passed before she found out. Yo' mama was a wildcat. Fit to be tied. Joan ripped up the clothes she kept for him in a drawer, called him all kinds of bastards and took you and moved. Hall shoulda come clean. Told Joan the truth. But Hall wanted his cake and eat it too."

"Well, why didn't she leave him?" Trudy asked, interested now. "He sounds like an asshole to me."

"Oh, she tried. One time she even stayed with me." Tony smiled at himself. He was almost embarrassed. He'd never told anyone he'd been with Joan. He always felt Joan was out of his class. He didn't want any of his friends to clown him. "But your mother was hooked. Couldn't pry herself loose. But there was something else too. Downright pitiful, if you ask me. See, Joan used to like messing with Hall's wife. She knew people at General Electric and had them cut off the woman's lights or disconnect her water. Bullshit stuff like calling her and hanging up late at night. She used to laugh this insane laugh and tell me about it. She told me it felt like she was stealing something valuable from that woman, but I could see underneath. Saw the lines in her face grow. I could see underneath she was dying."

"And after six years she's still on the creep," Trudy said.

"And it eats at your mother a little bit each day. I tell you, she ain't the same woman I knew. Your mama used to be the sunniest thing walking. Men used to line up just to see her. She was fine and carried herself proud. Any man would have been happy to have her."

Tony's wide smile slowly turned into a frown. "Ol' girl got a serious chip now."

Tony was right. Bitterness had turned Joan's injured heart to stone. She'd been longing for Hall for over seventeen years. The last six aged her the most. When he married that church girl, Joan felt stabbed in the gut. But even in anger, Joan stayed determined. She'd been waiting so long, so when Hall promised her he'd leave his wife as soon as Trudy was grown, Joan couldn't wait to get Trudy out.

"And after all this waiting, she's got a new worry now. She's afraid Mr. Hall's eyes will stray."

"Shoot, she doesn't look too worried to me. Besides, Mr. Hall gives her everything she wants. You'd think she'd be happy, not some mean, stuck-up rake."

Tony closed his eyes. Shook his head at the ground. "Junk food, whiskey, a blouse or a dress, a house down the street from a bar! Hall gave her everything but dignity and respect. He cheapened your mother, if you ask me." Tony gathered his papers and walked toward the door. "There were plenty of men who'd have given her that and a hell of a lot more." Tony looked out the window a real long time. "Your mama sold herself off too cheap."

"She's mean," Trudy said. "That's all I know."

"She ain't mean. She just mad at herself. You was just the only one there."

*Well, I'm getting out,* Trudy said to herself. She glared at the ripped couch and the old crates that served as his shelves. "I'm glad I'm not like her. I'm totally different."

Tony let his eyes roam over her dress. "Y'all act the same, if you ask me."

Trudy couldn't see any similarity at all. She didn't notice they both sashayed when they walked. Strutting down the street like a loud, blaring siren. Looking fearless, like they wore a bulletproof vest, parting the street like a sharp fine-tooth comb.

She was definitely on the same path as her mama, unless she did something different.

Trudy fingered the police officer's card in her hand and then ripped it up, tossing it in the trash.

# 21

## *Trudy and Vernita*

Trudy watched Tony walk down the street with slumped shoulders. A homeless man peed against the graffiti-filled wall. Tony stepped right in the wet.

Trudy picked up the phone and dialed Vernita.

"I thought I could leave early, but Tony busted me this time."

"Girl, yo' ass be taking some chances. You know I talked to Earl when I picked up my car. He told me his brother Junior got shot the other day."

"Junior! That quiet old man? He never bothered a soul."

"Earl said Junior was closing and a man driving a big black SUV wheeled up and blasted Junior's face."

"Damn. Junior was cool. That's exactly why I'm leaving the state."

"I know. It's the fucking Wild West, chile. These fools out here don't play," Vernita said.

"That's why we got to gank them fools first. Now listen. I got a hundred. I'll bring another over later. Keep picking Lil Steve's brain and planting them seeds. I want to know everything he's thinking."

"Girl, don't sweat it. I'm on the job." Vernita never had so much fun making money. She thought Trudy was crazy for paying her to be with Lil Steve. She'd have fucked that fine brotha for free. "Guess what that boy told me the other day about Ray Ray?"

Suddenly the second line rang. "Hold on," Trudy told Vernita.

"Dee's Parlor, I mean, Tony's," Trudy said, answering the phone.

"Hello, songbird. How did you sleep last night?"

Trudy recognized Jimmy's deep, resonant voice.

"I just wanted to know one thing," Jimmy said and stopped.

Trudy's heart skipped a beat. Does he know something already? "What?" Trudy said, holding her breath.

"Is the sun shining on your street like it's shining on mine?"

Trudy smiled while holding her mouth close

to the phone. "It looks real good from down here," she said.

"What time do you get off, baby?"

"My friend's supposed to come pick me up but I have a couple more things to finish first."

"Tell your friend you have a ride. I'll be there at three-fifteen."

He hung up the phone before Trudy could protest. She went back to the first line.

"Dang, you have people on hold a long time," Vernita said when Trudy clicked back. "Who were you talking to so long?"

"This guy I met at the club."

"The club? Girl, I thought you learned your lesson last time."

In the ten months Trudy had been on her own she'd already had a nice share of guys.

"This one is different. He's a tad on the thug-gish side but he's hellified rich. You'd be jealous as hell if you saw him," Trudy said.

"He ain't the brother from the other night, is he?"

"You saw him? I thought you'd left."

"I was half out the door when he asked you to dance. Girl, Pearl pulled my coat about that crazy-ass brother. I know you're not trying to tangle with no drug-dealin' fool! Don't act crazy. Homeboy's in a whole 'nother league, hear? Yo' ass is bound to get played."

"Not unless I play him first," Trudy said back.

But Vernita was worried. She sucked against

her teeth. "Girlfriend, stop trippin'! You're bad at judging men. 'Member when Baxter was after yo' ass?"

"Yeah." Trudy laughed at the memory. "He gave me those thigh-high suede boots."

"They were used!" Vernita reminded her friend. "Probably snatched 'em off some other chick's legs."

"Baxter was cool, just a little eccentric."

"Eccentric? He left a dead cat at your door! I know you didn't forget about that! Listen, girl, I'm telling you, homeboy's no joke." When Trudy didn't respond, Vernita kept talking. "I know you hear me. Look, don't be no fool. You ain't been on your own for that long. You had a couple of silly-ass boys and suddenly you think you're grown."

Although Trudy was living alone and taking care of herself, Vernita thought she was getting too fast. "This here's a full-fledged grown, drug-dealing man! Please tell me he's not in this shit you pulled me in. That boy's a heart attack walking."

Trudy didn't tell her he was part of the bank plan too. "You worry too much. Can we please change the subject?"

"Change the subject? Girl, you about to change your whole life!"

"All right, all right! Don't get so excited. I'm just playing with him, that's all. Teasing him a bit. I'm telling you, he doesn't know shit, Vernita. He doesn't even know that I work at the bank. He'd never suspect it was us."

"Us? I'm about to be out this bitch now!"

"Come on, Vernita. Just listen a minute. We ain't the ones that'll be doing the work. That's Lil Steve's job. He handles the drama. All we do is hit him."

Vernita was quiet. She didn't like this at all. "That's what I was about to tell you before you put me on hold. Lil Steve was the one who turned Ray Ray in."

"What?" Trudy asked, amazed. "Are you telling the truth?"

"He gave him up to avoid going to jail himself. Damn, girl, now you know that shit's cold. I told you these fools are treacherous. Don't think they're not; they just ain't aimed their big guns at you yet," Vernita said. "I'm telling you, I really don't know about this job. This shit's getting a little too deep."

Trudy thought long and hard about what Vernita said. Now she was really concerned about Ray Ray. But it just made her more determined than ever to pay Lil Steve back.

"Look, don't you want your shop? Own the whole thing outright? Don't you want to kick backstabbing Keesha to the curb?"

"I'd rather kick yo' ass for taking dumb chances."

"Vernita, please don't trip. Our part is safe. Besides, you'll be wearing a disguise."

"I'd rather be alive in my rusty-ass shop than die because my silly-ass friend got too greedy. This man is dangerous, Trudy! Didn't you hear what Pearl said? You gonna fuck around and end up like you did in March."

Trudy knew what Vernita was talking about. Two months ago, Trudy had dated Roger, a boxer. She still couldn't sleep on one side.

"I'll be safe," Trudy told her. "My friend at the LAPD can have him checked out. You just worry about Lil Steve."

Trudy remembered what the cop told her when she had him look up Roger.

"Listen," the cop had said, studying Trudy's young face. "If you have to come down and run a make on a brother, you must be messing around with the wrong one."

**"If you have to come down and make on a brother, you must be messing around with the wrong one," the police tell Trudy. Vernita thinks Trudy is bad at judging men. With the robbery days away, is Jimmy a killer? Can Charles be trusted with the money? Will Lil Steve's addiction put them in jeapordy? Find out in part two, *Get Some*.**

253

*The most lethal ride-or-die women in Memphis now run their gangs and the streets. But the aftermath of an all-out war means merciless new enemies, time-bomb secrets . . . and one chance to take it all . . .*

## BOSS DIVAS

Available September 2014 wherever books and ebooks are sold.

# 1

## *Ta'Shara*

"STOP THE FUCKING CAR!"

Profit slams on the brakes while I bolt out of the passenger car door and race into the night toward my foster parents' burning house.

"TRACEE! REGGIE!" *They're not in there. Please, God. Don't let them be in there.* "TRACEE! REGGIE!"

"Ta'Shara, wait up," Profit yells. His long strides eat up the distance between us even as I shove my way through the city's emergency responders. I've never seen flames stretch so high or felt such intense heat. Still, none of that shit stopped me. In my delusional mind, there is still time to get them out of there.

"Hey, lady. You can't go in there," someone shouts and makes a grab for me.

As I draw closer to the front porch, Profit is

able to wrap one of his powerful arms around my waist and lift me off my feet. "Baby, stop. You can't go in there."

"Let me go!" My legs pedal in the air as I stretch uselessly for the door. "TRACEE! REGGIE!" My screams rake my throat raw.

Profit drags me away from the growing flames.

Men in uniform rush over to us. I don't know who they are and I don't care. I just need to know one thing. "Where are my parents? Did they make it out?"

"Ma'am, calm down. Please tell me your name."

"WHERE ARE THEY?"

"Ma'am—"

"ANSWER ME, DAMMIT!"

"C'mon, man," Profit says. "Give my girl something."

The fireman draws a deep breath and then drops a bomb that changes my life forever.

"The neighbors reported the fire. Right now, I'm not aware of anyone making it out of the house. I'm sorry."

"NOOOOOOO!" I collapse in Profit's arm. He hauls me up against his six-three frame and I lay my head on his broad chest. Before, I found comfort in his strong embrace, but not tonight. I sob uncontrollably as pain overwhelms me, but then I make out a familiar car down the street.

"Oh. My. God."

Profit tenses. "What?"

My eyes aren't deceiving me. Sitting behind the wheel of her burgundy Crown Victoria is LeShelle, with a slow smile creeping across her face. She forms a gun with her hand and pretends to fire at us.

*We're next.*

LeShelle tosses back her head and, despite the siren's wail, the roaring fire, and the chaos around me, that bitch's maniacal laugh rings in my ears.

*How much more of this shit am I going to take? When will this fuckin' bullshit end?*

*BOOM!*

The crowd gasps while windows explode from the top floor of the house, but my gaze never waivers from LeShelle. My tears dry up as anger grips me.

She did this shit. I don't need a jury to tell me that the bitch is guilty as hell. How long has she been threatening the Douglases' lives? Why in the hell didn't I believe that she would follow through?

LeShelle has proven her ruthlessness time after time. This fucking Gangster Disciples versus the Vice Lords shit ain't a game to her. It's a way of life. And she doesn't give a fuck who she hurts.

My blood boils and all at once everything

burst out of me. I wrench away from Profit's protective arms and take off toward LeShelle in a rage.

"I'M GOING TO FUCKING KILL YOU!"

"TA'SHARA, NO!" Profit shouts.

I ignore him as I race toward LeShelle's car. My hot tears burn tracks down my face.

LeShelle laughs in my face and then pulls off from the curb, but not before I'm able to pound my fist against the trunk.

Profit's arms wrap back around my waist, but I kick out and connect with LeShelle's taillight and shatter that mutherfucka. The small wave of satisfaction I get is quickly erased when her piece of shit car burps out a black cloud of exhaust in my face.

"NO! Don't let her get away. No!"

"Ta'Shara, please. Not now. Let it go!"

*Let it go?* I round on Profit. "How the fuck can you say that shit?"

*BOOM!*

More windows explode, drawing my attention back to the only place that I've ever called home. My heart claws its way out of my chest as orange flames and black smoke lick the sky.

My legs give out and my knees kiss the concrete, all the while Profit's arms remain locked around me. I can't hear what he's saying because my sobs drown him out.

"This is all my fault," tumbles over my tongue.

I conjure up an image of Tracee and Reggie: the last time I'd seen them. It's a horrible memory. Everyone was angry and everyone said things that . . . they can never be taken back.

Grief consumes me. I squeeze my eyes tight and cling to the ghosts inside of my head. "I'm sorry. I'm so sorry."

Profit's arms tighten. I melt in his arms even though I want to lash out. *Isn't it his fault for my foster parents roasting in that house, too?* When the question crosses my mind I crumble from the weight of my shame.

I'm to blame. No one else.

A heap in the center of the street, I lay my head against Profit's chest again and take in the horrific sight through a steady sheen of tears. The Douglases were good people. All they wanted was the best for me and for me to believe in myself. They would've done the same for LeShelle if she'd given them the chance.

LeShelle fell in love with the streets and the make-believe power of being the head bitch of the Queen Gs. I didn't want anything to do with any of that bullshit, but it didn't matter. I'm viewed as GD property by blood, and the shit hit the fan when I fell in love with Profit—a Vice Lord by blood. Back then Profit wasn't a soldier yet. But our being together was taken as a sign of disrespect. LeShelle couldn't let it slide.

However, the harder I fight the streets' politics, the more I'm dragged down into her bull-shit world of gangs and violence.

"I should have killed her when I had the chance." If I had Tracee and Reggie would still be alive. "She won't get away with this," I vow. "I'm going to kill her if it's the last thing I do."